A Teaspoon of Trouble

A Teaspoon of Trouble

A Bachelor Bake-Off Romance

Shirley Jump

TULE
PUBLISHING

Chapter One

T HE DOG WAS going to be a problem.

Carolyn Hanson stared at the dog. He stared back, tail swishing against the white tile floor in a fast semicircle. Hopeful, friendly, determined. "What am I supposed to do with you?"

"We gotta take him, Aunt Carolyn." Her niece Emma put a protective hand on the dog's collar. "Roscoe is my puppy and I love him."

Puppy was being used loosely, considering the dog weighed at least fifty pounds and stood three feet off the ground. He was some kind of mutt mix, with a square boxer face and big ears: one that flopped to the right, one that stood straight up. He seemed like a nice enough dog, so far not much of a barker or jumper, but Carolyn was most definitely not a dog person.

She wasn't a kid person, either, but that hadn't stopped her sister from naming her as Emma's guardian when a car accident took both Sandy and her husband Bob in one fell swoop.

Sandy. The thought of her late sister shot a hot river of searing grief through Carolyn's chest. Almost a month ago, a drunk driver had crossed the median, slamming headfirst into Sandy and Bob's car. They'd been out on a rare date, something Sandy had been looking forward to all week. And just like that, they were gone, and their only child, a precocious four-year-old named Emma who Carolyn had only met a handful of times, was now…

Her responsibility.

For a woman who regularly worked eighty hours a week as a sous chef at a busy restaurant in Manhattan, raising a kid and a "puppy" was going to be impossible. She lived in a tiny cramped apartment of a five-story walk-up in the meatpacking district. So she had asked her boss for a two-week leave of absence so she could pick up Emma and go back home to Montana and figure out a plan.

Plans gave her comfort, direction, structure. She knew what time she was going to get up, what time she'd get to work, which day she would do laundry, which day she'd grocery shop—everything was listed in little bullets on the running list on her refrigerator at home.

What she hadn't planned for was a four-year-old and a dog. Why had her sister thought Carolyn would make a good guardian? She worked into the wee hours of the mornings, lived as sparsely as possible, hadn't had a real relationship in two years, and had always vowed she'd never get married or have kids. If there was a list of the top 100 people who should be Emma's guardian, Carolyn would be number 101.

After the accident, Bob's parents—who lived just two towns away—had taken Emma and the dog. Then the lawyer had called Carolyn and told her she had been named guardian. Bob's parents were in their late seventies and overwhelmed by the addition of a small child and a dog to their home, and as sad as they were to see Emma go, Carolyn could almost feel their relief. That left Carolyn in charge, the least motherly person in her family.

The dog's tail swooped across the floor, back and forth. Sandy's house was much like Sandy herself had been—comfortably messy and warm. Toys littered the floor, photos perched on every available surface, and the air smelled of cinnamon and sugar.

Sandy had loved being a mom, loved everything about the experience. She read the books at night, went to the Mommy & Me classes, did the long days at the playground and the afternoons under tents made out of sheets and couch cushions. Every conversation Carolyn had with her sister had been about Emma, as if everything else in Sandy's life disappeared the minute she gave birth. It was a concept so foreign to Carolyn, it might as well have been another language.

So now she stood in the sunny yellow kitchen of Sandy's house, missing her sister with an ache that ran deep and sharp, and wondered what the hell she was going to do.

"I love my puppy," Emma said and wrapped her arms around Roscoe's neck. "*Please*, Aunt Carolyn?"

It was the *please* that got her in the end. Emma had lost her family and was now having to leave the only home she'd ever known. Carolyn looked down at the little blond girl, bouncy ringlets surrounding a cherubic face and big blue eyes. Ever since Sandy had died, Emma had taken to carrying around one of Sandy's sweaters. She held it now, clutched between her and the dog, the red knit standing out like a beacon. Emma's eyes welled and her lower lip trembled.

Carolyn thought of the suitcases in the hall, all of Emma's life reduced to two wheeled bags. Once Carolyn had figured out a permanent solution, she'd come back and deal with the house and the furniture, but for now, all Emma had was two suitcases, a thick sweater, and Roscoe. How could Carolyn possibly ask her to leave her dog behind, too?

How bad could it be, right? Besides, she'd be at her parents' house in Marietta. Surely they could help with Emma and with the dog. Do whatever it was that a dog needed. She was going to have to figure out how to get a dog from Wyoming to Montana, along with her niece and all the luggage in the same car, but surely it was doable.

She bent down to Emma's level, but stayed a little to the right of the dog. He looked like he wanted to lick Carolyn's face or crawl into her lap. "Okay, Emma, we'll take him with us."

Emma's smile spread wide and fast. She jumped forward,

wrapping Carolyn in a tight hug. "Thank you, thank you, thank you!"

"You're…" Carolyn drew back a bit, awkward with this whole kid thing, a kid she barely knew, a kid who hugged everything from the dog to the sofa, "…welcome."

"And then when Mommy comes home, I can tell her all about Roscoe going to Grandma's house," Emma said.

"Your mom…" Carolyn struggled to find the words. Hadn't Bob's parents had this talk with Emma already? How could Emma still not know, all this time later? Were they just waiting for Carolyn to have this talk? Carolyn, the last person on earth who knew how to comfort a grieving child? "Your mom…isn't coming home, Emma."

"Yes, she is." Emma crossed her arms over her chest. "Stop saying she's not."

Carolyn had talked to a friend who was a psychologist last week, when she'd found out about Emma. Carolyn had never had to deal with a kid, and needed advice on how to handle the whole transition thing. *She'll accept the truth when she's ready*, the psychologist had said. *Don't push it.*

"We need to finish packing for your trip to Grandma Marilyn's," Carolyn said. Maybe if she distracted Emma with something to do, it would erase that sad but defiant look in her eyes. Carolyn only had a couple hours before they needed to get on the road—which meant Carolyn needed to find a way to transport that puppy to Montana.

More and more, it looked like the most likely option was

putting Roscoe in the back of her SUV and driving him. Carolyn could only picture her seats shredded and gnawed. Was there some kind of state-to-state dog delivery service? "So, what do you want to take for food in the car?"

"Spaghetti."

"Uh, we can't take that in the car. It's pretty messy."

"Spaghetti is my favorite. Roscoe likes it too."

Carolyn let out a breath. "How about we have something else? Like a sandwich. Do you want a sandwich?"

"Mommy makes me san-wiches," Emma said. "I want Mommy's san-wich."

"She…she can't do that right now," Carolyn said. "Just tell me what your mommy puts in the sandwich and I'll make the same thing."

Emma shook her head. "I want Mommy to do it." Then her cheeks reddened, tears filled her eyes and ran down her face in fast rivers. "I don't want you to do it. I want Mommy to."

Carolyn stood there, feeling helpless, wishing Emma's grandparents were here or Sandy was here, or anyone at all, to help explain the situation to Emma. She got down to Emma's level again. Change the subject, reroute Emma back to something else. "We're going to Grandma Marilyn's house today. Isn't that going to be fun?"

Emma's lower lip trembled. She held Carolyn's gaze for one long second, then glanced at the floor. She clutched the sweater close to her chest. "I don't wanna go. I wanna stay here."

Carolyn sighed. She had no idea how to make this better, how to help Emma. Except to take her to Montana where hopefully Carolyn's parents could handle her better than Carolyn could. She kept her eye on that destination. "We can't do that, Emma. But we're going to take your dog, and we're going to see Grandma, and it's going to be fun. I promise."

Although Carolyn had no idea what made for fun with a four-year-old, or how all these changes in the little girl's life could possibly be labeled as fun. It just sounded like the right thing to say.

"I don't wanna go!" Emma turned on her heel and ran out of the room. A second later, there was the slam of a door.

Or maybe "it's going to be fun" was the absolutely wrong thing to say. Carolyn sighed.

Just when she thought she'd escape unscathed, the dog leaned over and licked Carolyn's face, leaving a trail of slobber from her chin to her temple. It was going to be one long trip to Montana.

MATTHEW WEST HAD seen three pregnant cats before lunch. Was there some kind of pregnant cat epidemic in Marietta that he had missed? Or more likely, Mrs. George's randy tomcat had had one hell of a night on the town a few months ago. The frisky orange tiger was known for being a busy bachelor cat. Matt cradled the gray tabby in his arms, then headed out to his front office. He'd set up his veterinary practice in Marietta six years ago, after going away for college, an experience that confirmed there was nowhere else in the world he'd rather be than this quaint, warm town. His office faced the Java Café, the two of them on opposite sides of 3rd Street, which meant he always had the scent of fresh coffee and baked muffins wafting in through the windows. Between him and Emory Bishop, the large-animal vet, creatures great and small were covered in Marietta.

"And who belongs to this little girl?" he said, giving the tabby a tender rub on the head.

Brooklyn Murphy popped to her feet. She was eight years old, dressed head to toe in pink, her long brown hair held in place by a sparkly pink headband. Her mother, Meg, sat beside her on the orange vinyl chair. "Me!" Brooklyn said. "That's my cat Milly."

"Well," Matt said, bending down to Brooklyn's level, "Miss Milly here isn't sick. She's actually going to…" he glanced up at Meg, "…be a mom."

Brooklyn's eyes widened. "She's gonna have kittens?"

Meg gasped. "Wait, she's pregnant?"

"Yup. And in about four weeks, you're going to have a few little ones. I counted four, but sometimes there's one hiding back there." He always loved this moment, the adventure and excitement of a new life. It made up for all the days when he had to deliver sad news to a pet lover, and the stressful days when it seemed he had more patients than time.

"Kittens." Meg sighed. Matt could see her already calculating the extra chaos a bunch of kittens would bring to her house. Meg was already involved in an animal rescue program that had placed a lot of strays in town with good families. This particular stray, Milly, had stolen Brooklyn's heart and become part of the family.

"I can take care of them," Brooklyn said. "I'll love them and feed them."

"Their mom is going to do a lot of that, Brooklyn," Matt said. "When they're big enough, you can bring them here and your mom and I can find them some great homes."

Brooklyn pouted. "But I don't wanna give them away."

"Whoever adopts one of these kittens—when they're old enough—is going to love them as much as you do and treat them extra special. Do you remember how happy people are when they adopt from your rescue program? That's how they're going to feel about these kittens. Plus, I bet you're going to be able to visit them and play with them whenever you want," Matt said. That was the good thing about a small town. People here all knew each other, and treated each other like family.

Relief filled Meg's features. "Sounds like a plan. Thanks, Dr. West."

"Anytime." He handed the cat to Brooklyn, and gave the

tabby one more pat. "Take good care of her and make sure she gets plenty of rest."

"I will! I promise!" They crossed to the counter, paid the bill, then headed out the door, Brooklyn chatting the whole way about the new kittens and what she wanted to name them. Matt chuckled. Yup, it was a good day in the office.

Matt crossed to the small window beside the receptionist's desk. "What's next, Sheryl?"

"Just one more for the day, and then we're done." She handed him a chart. Brunette and stout, Sheryl was organized, efficient and friendly, and a total pushover for anything with four paws. She'd been his receptionist since day one, and he couldn't imagine running his office without her. "Oh, and Jane McCullough dropped this off this morning. Don't forget the Bake-Off is next weekend."

Matt groaned. He *had* forgotten about that, even though he'd signed up as one of the sponsors, and then gotten talked into signing up as one of the bachelors who had to bake on stage. A marketing ploy, Jane had assured him, to get more attention from the media and a friendly amount of bidding from the single women in town. All for a good cause, too— to benefit the drive to fund something to memorialize Harry Monroe, who'd died back in September.

Matt had known first responder Harry Monroe pretty well. The twenty-seven-year-old had been killed on Highway 89 a few months ago, after he'd stopped to help an elderly couple change a flat tire. His family, who owned the grocery store in town, were well respected, but also grieving over the loss of their son, as was the rest of the town.

The Chamber of Commerce had the idea of turning an empty house in town into a community center for kids and teens—a cause dear to Harry's heart—and they'd come up with the Bachelor Bake-Off as a way to raise money to renovate the house. There was a time crunch, too, since an investment company was looking at buying the property. Pretty much everyone in Crawford County wanted to see Harry memorialized with a boys' and girls' center, hence the Bake-Off, part of a series of fundraisers.

Matt hadn't hesitated when Jane, who worked for the Chamber of Commerce, proposed the idea. In 1914, the town had done something similar to draw attention to the reopening of the Graff Hotel. The Bake-Off was part of what Matt loved about Marietta—how the town worked like a big hug—and what had made him insanely agree to participate in a bachelor bake-off fundraiser.

Problem? He couldn't bake. The last time he'd bought one of those ready-made tubes of cookie dough, he'd ended up with an oozing burnt glob on the bottom of his stove. Six months later, and he could still catch the scent of burned chocolate chips whenever he opened the oven to warm up a pizza.

"So, what are you going to bake?" Sheryl asked.

"Cookies from the supermarket." He grinned. "Think I can get away with that?"

"Uh, considering it's a live, on a stage baking contest…no." Sheryl shook her head and smirked. "All I can say is good luck and I'm going to be in the front row, watching you crash and burn. Because I'm a good friend like that."

"Gee, thanks. Remind me to dock your pay next week."

Sheryl laughed. "Go ahead. Maybe you can put it toward a lucky charm for the Bake-Off."

"I don't need luck. I have skills." He grinned again, then turned his attention to the chart. One more patient and his day was done. He flipped through the sheets, a quick scan of the facts about his patient, a dog—mutt, fifty pounds, with a complaint of him acting out and not eating. Matt came around the corner and entered the waiting room. "Roscoe?"

A blonde in the corner looked up from the magazine she was reading, and when her green eyes connected with his, his heart did a familiar skip-beat. He knew those eyes. Knew that blonde. Even in a thick winter coat, he could recognize her from ten miles away. Holy hell. What was she doing back in town? "Carolyn?"

The dog popped up, as did a little girl, maybe four years old, with blond ringlets and big green eyes. Carolyn's daughter? Was she married?

And why did that thought disappoint him? He hadn't seen her in ten years, since senior year of high school, since the day she left him in her rearview mirror. *I want more than this small-town life*, she'd said. *I want more than…*

Us. That was the word she had left unsaid. The word

that had stung.

He cleared his throat. Went for cool, casual, you-didn't-break-my-heart. "Hey, Carolyn."

She gave him a little nod. Also going for cool and casual, but more in the we-hardly-knew-each-other way. "Hey, Matt."

From the exchange, no one would know that he had once been wildly in love with her. That his entire world had centered around her, and her smile. And how the day of graduation, their paths had diverged and he had realized he had never really known the girl he had loved. Ancient history. Which was where his thoughts about her should stay.

The dog—a boxer mix with a friendly tail, lunged as far forward as the leash would allow, nosing into Matt's pant leg. Carolyn let out an oomph, and stood, trying to rein the dog back in, but he was stronger than her and she skidded several steps forward, while the dog plowed into Matt's legs.

"Sorry." Carolyn let out a gust. "That dog is…disobedient. And stubborn."

Matt grinned. "Sometimes the dog takes his cue from the owner."

"I'm not his owner. Well, I am, but…" She let out another gust and brushed her bangs back. "It's complicated."

Complicated. What did that mean and why was he spending any mental energy trying to figure that out? Ancient history, he reminded himself again.

Matt bent down and gave the dog an ear rub. The dog's tail went into happy frenzy mode, and he gave Matt's hand a lick. "Hey there, buddy. What's the problem?"

Much easier to deal with the dog than whatever history still existed between him and Carolyn.

The little girl stood next to her dog, a protective hand on his collar. "Roscoe's sick. He doesn't want to eat. I think he has a tummy-ache."

"And he's about as obedient as a two-year-old," Carolyn muttered. She was still trying to wrangle the dog, but Roscoe pulled away, twining his leash around Matt's legs.

Matt glanced at the little girl. Worry filled her face and furrowed her brow. "I'm sure Roscoe's just fine, but I'm gonna take a look at him and make sure. Okay?"

"Uh-huh," the little girl said. "My name is Emma and I'm four."

Matt chuckled. He put out his hand. "I'm Dr. West, but you can call me Dr. Matt. Nice to meet you, Emma." She gave him a serious little handshake. Cute kid.

He was still shocked Carolyn had a child. Matt had always wanted kids. Wendy, his ex-wife, had talked about having them, too, then a year into their marriage she'd changed her mind. The divorce was two years in the past, and although Matt was relieved the marriage had ended, he still wished he'd become a father.

Given how polite and well-mannered Emma was, Carolyn must be a good mother. He'd always thought she was more driven by her career than by family, and that she had been clear she never wanted to settle down and have kids. Maybe he hadn't known her as well as he thought. Or maybe she just hadn't wanted to settle down with *him*.

"All right, Roscoe, let's get started." Matt stepped deftly out of the leash loop, then opened the door that led to the exam rooms and ushered Carolyn, the dog, and Carolyn's daughter into the hall. "Exam Room One, the first door on your right."

Roscoe led the way, dragging Carolyn behind him. When the dog found the rear second exit of the exam room blocked by a closed door, he stood in the center of the small exam space, panting and wagging his tail. Carolyn put a hand on Emma's shoulder and steered her into a seat. "Emma, you need to sit down and be quiet, okay? So the doctor can look at that dog."

"But…but…I got questions. About Roscoe."

"Questions are great, Emma," Matt said. "They help you learn."

"My mommy says I'm smart." Emma beamed.

"Emma, please sit down," Carolyn said. "Let the doctor do his job."

Strange. He'd expected Carolyn to brag about Emma or agree that she was smart.

"Okay." Emma sank onto the bench, and propped her chin up on her hands. Carolyn took off her winter coat, and set it on the bench beside Emma. Matt did his best not to check Carolyn out.

And failed.

"All right, Emma. Let's see how Roscoe is doing." Matt bent down, and hoisted the dog up and onto the stainless steel table. As he did, he couldn't help but notice Carolyn's legs: long and lean, defined by a pair of blue jeans that still hugged all the right places. She had on short black leather boots with a little bit of a heel. Hot and sexy. Damn.

The dog scrambled a bit against the cool, slippery surface, but Matt ran a hand down his neck and whispered a few soothing words. "It's okay, buddy, just chill." Roscoe quieted into complacency, not entirely happy about the foreign surface below his paws, but not fighting it anymore either.

"How do you do that?" Carolyn said. "I haven't been able to get that dog to sit still for a week."

"You just gotta know how to handle him. How to send out the vibes that it's okay to relax, and that you're the boss."

Carolyn scoffed. "Easier said than done, apparently, because he doesn't listen to me. At all."

Matt swung his stethoscope around and pressed it to the dog's heart. Nice, strong heartbeat. He palpated the dog's belly, checked his teeth and eyes. All good. As much as he wanted to ask Carolyn why she was back in town, he kept on focusing on the dog. Then he wouldn't notice Carolyn's deep green eyes, or the graceful curve of her neck, or the fact that his own heart was racing a bit right now.

"Whatcha doing?" Emma asked, getting to her feet.

Carolyn waved at the little girl. "Emma, sit down; you don't want to get in the doctor's way."

"She's okay. I'm checking his belly, Emma. And listening to his heart. Here, you want to try it?" He waved her over, and put the stethoscope into her ears, then pressed the other end to the dog's chest. "Hear that? It's Roscoe's heartbeat."

Emma's eyes widened. Matt always loved seeing that little moment of discovery and joy when he got kids involved with his work. "It's really fast," Emma said.

"Yup. And that's good. Dogs' hearts beat about twice as fast as ours do. Wanna see?"

Emma nodded. Matt bent down and pressed the stethoscope to Emma's chest. "Do you hear your heart?"

Emma nodded. "Roscoe's is faster!"

"Pretty cool, huh?" He straightened again, then turned to Carolyn, keeping his demeanor the same as he would with any other owner. "Tell me what's making him get sick."

"I don't know." Carolyn shrugged. "I bought him dog food and all he does is throw it up."

"Did you buy the same kind he always ate?"

"I don't know what kind he always ate." She shrugged again. "I forgot to bring it with me, and there was no way I was driving back to Wyoming when there was Alpo at the store."

He kept on looking at the dog, because every time his gaze went to Carolyn, his heart did that same skip-beat. She had let her hair grow longer, and it curled around her shoulders. She still had the same elegant features he remembered. He knew if she put her hair up, that he would be able to see the long lines of her neck, the curve of her shoulders. When they'd been together, his favorite place to kiss her was in that small divot at the base of her neck. Just thinking about that sent his mind down some southern paths.

Matt cleared his throat. Focus on the dog, not on her, or why she was back in town. "Uh, sometimes a big change in food will cause a dog to get sick. The best thing you can do is mix the new food in gradually with his old food. You don't remember the brand he ate?"

"He's not even my dog. And I can't ask his owners."

"I'm sure you could text them or—"

"I can't." Tears welled in her eyes but she steeled herself and they disappeared. She put a protective hand on Emma's shoulder. "So please just tell me what to do to get him to stop puking all over the house, and to listen better."

What was that about? Why was Carolyn teary? He wanted to ask, but the days when he could do that had passed long ago. Something was off with Carolyn, something was upsetting her, but he had lost the right to ask why ten years ago.

"I, uh, can put Roscoe here on an easy-digestion diet," Matt said. "That should help. As for the training, if you work with him, you can get him to curb his behaviors. I can give you a great book on training."

Carolyn blew a lock of hair out of her eyes. "I am not a dog person. At all," she said, lowering her voice and leaning closer to him. That gave him a view of the swell of her breasts beneath the V of her coral T-shirt.

And he forgot to breathe.

"I'm a chef," she went on. "I can cook or bake anything, but I can't train a dog. So if you could point me in the direction of the nearest professional trainer…"

Matt chuckled. "This is Marietta. You know how small this town is. It's not like we are overrun with dog trainers."

"He's chewed up my shoes, dug a tunnel to China in the backyard, and when I say come, he runs the other way. I spent the better part of yesterday going up and down the streets looking for him. I need someone to give this dog a little law and order."

A part of him felt bad for Carolyn. She was clearly stressed, and needed some help with the dog. He wondered where the dog had come from, how Carolyn had ended up with it, and why she was back in town with a four-year-old. He hadn't seen her in ten years, but she still looked beautiful. That, and the clear need in her voice, spurred him to want to help.

Clearly, he was a glutton for punishment.

"Let me draw a little blood, rule out anything else with his tummy issues, and see where we go from there. Okay?" He turned to grab a needle out of the drawer, then swabbed a spot on Roscoe's front leg, inserted the needle, and withdrew some blood.

"Is that gonna hurt Roscoe?" Emma asked.

"Nope. He won't even notice it," Matt said, then pulled the needle out, held a fresh gauze pad on the leg for a moment to stop the bleeding, and gave Roscoe another ear rub. The dog leaned into his touch, groaning. "This dog is a pushover. Maybe a little rambunctious because he's young, but still a total marshmallow."

Carolyn scoffed. "Pushover? Marshmallow? It's like he's a whole other dog with you," she said. "Maybe he hates me."

Emma parked her fists on her hips. "Roscoe loves everyone, Aunt Carolyn."

Aunt Carolyn? As in maybe Sandy's daughter, not Carolyn's? Matt remembered Carolyn's older sister well. She'd been a couple years ahead of them in high school, more easygoing and sociable than headstrong, driven Carolyn, but always nice to him in those days when he'd pretty much camped out on Carolyn's doorstep.

He wasn't surprised Sandy had children. She'd been in Girl Scouts and 4-H and had always seemed the type who would settle down with a nice banker or something and raise a family in a little white picket fence house. Of course, there was always the possibility of Emma being an in-law niece, but Matt didn't think so. The family features were too similar.

And that thought brought him right back to Carolyn's eyes and her smile, and all the things he was trying not to think about. Still, he found himself checking her left hand for a wedding ring—none. Didn't mean Carolyn wasn't married but did up the odds that she was still single.

Ancient history. Stop thinking about it.

"Let me go get that dog food for you," Matt said. Focus on his job, not on whatever was going on in Carolyn's life. "Blood test results will be back tomorrow, but I don't think there'll be anything other than a change in diet that got Roscoe a little off-kilter."

He lowered Roscoe back onto the floor and handed the leash to Carolyn. When he did, their hands brushed, and a little electric thrill ran through him. Damn. All these years apart, and she still affected him.

Carolyn's eyes met his. "Thanks, Matt."

"No problem," he mumbled, then headed out of the room. He dropped the syringe into the testing bin, then darted into the storage room, and retrieved a bag of dog food. Down the hall, two of the dogs being boarded for the week started to bark.

On the other side of Exam Room One's back entrance door, Matt could hear Roscoe joining in on the barking with deep, throaty woofs. He opened the door, his arms full with the dog food bag, and Roscoe lunged forward, squeezing past Matt's legs and taking a quick left down the hall. Carolyn was right behind Roscoe, a death grip on the other end of the leash. She tried to skid to a stop, but ended up slamming into Matt's chest.

He dropped the bag to the floor, reached out and caught her around the waist, and for one brief second, they looked at each other, surprised, breathless. In the space of a heartbeat, he remembered everything from their relationship. The way she smiled. The way she used to lean into him at the end of the day. The way she made him laugh. Then Carolyn stepped back and Matt let go, and Roscoe made a break for it, charging down the hall toward the kennels.

Carolyn cursed. "That dog—"

"I got him. Don't worry." Matt broke into a light jog, caught up to Roscoe just as he reached the kennels. Matt grabbed the leash, gave it a slight tug. "Roscoe, no."

The dog looked back at Matt, tail wagging, his features saying, *please, please let me go see these new friends.*

Instead Matt turned on his heel, patted his leg, and gave the leash another gentle tug. "Come, Roscoe." The dog gave the kennels one last longing look, then obeyed.

Emma was peeking around the door of Exam Room One. She broke into a run when she saw Roscoe approaching, and buried her face in his neck. "Don't run away, Roscoe. 'Kay?"

Carolyn shot Roscoe an irritated glare. "I swear, that dog is going to be the end of me. Thank you."

"No problem. He just wanted to make some new friends." Matt held the leash out to her but she didn't take it. Instead, she leaned against the jamb and crossed her arms over her chest.

"I have an offer for you."

Matt arched a brow. "Offer?"

"I saw this on the counter when you were gone." She held up the Bake-Off flyer. "If I remember right, you can barely make a grilled cheese sandwich."

Even his grilled cheese abilities were sketchy at best. Matt had takeout and microwave reheating mastered, though. "It was a good cause, to help honor the memory of a first responder who died recently. Do you remember Harry Monroe? He was killed in a hit and run on Highway 89 on Labor Day."

"That's terrible. He was such a nice guy." Carolyn shook her head. "I'm glad the town is doing something for him."

"All the money raised is going to renovate a house near the Chamber of Commerce to make it into a youth center. Something Harry would have loved." Matt took off his stethoscope and put it on the counter. "Anyway, my business is sponsoring the first night of the Bake-Off, and somehow that got me roped into baking too. I was hoping I could fake it."

Carolyn laughed. "You can't fake baking. But what you can do is a little…quid pro quo."

A smile twitched on his lips. Despite everything, Matt was intrigued. "Quid pro quo?"

"You train this incorrigible dog and I'll teach you how to bake." She flashed him a smile, a smile he knew as well as his own. Ten years later and that smile still had the power to affect him. "You have a week to learn how to create a dessert, and I have a week to figure out what I'm going to do with that dog and my job. So how about a little partnership?"

It was a crazy deal. Being around her for hours on end would be painful. Difficult. Impossible. So he said, "Sounds like a great idea."

Apparently some old dogs didn't learn their lessons.

Chapter Two

WHAT HAD MADE her propose such a crazy idea?

Desperation. That was the only possible answer. There was no other way she would have voluntarily signed up to work with Matthew West. Ten years ago, she'd thought the sun rose in his eyes every day. She'd dreamed of them being together forever.

Then he'd told her he had no intention of ever leaving Marietta. And she'd realized that all the plans she had would disappear if she stayed in that town, became the perfect little housewife until she rotted away in some rocking chair on her front porch. She'd wanted a bigger life than that, more than a little house in a quiet neighborhood. So she'd packed her bags and headed for New York the next day, vowing never to return to the small town that had always suffocated her.

Until now.

"Aunt Carolyn, that doctor was very nice." Emma said as she climbed into the booster seat in the back of Carolyn's SUV. Roscoe scrambled up beside Emma and settled on the seat, shaking fur and slush all over the black leather and ignoring the blanket Carolyn had laid on the floor. Yet another battle with the dog Carolyn had lost before she even crossed the Wyoming state line.

"Yes, he was." Very nice, and very handsome still. Matt had barely aged, and had the same lean, muscular frame she remembered. A little taller, a little broader, but with the same dark hair, brown eyes, and unforgettable smile. He was the quintessential small-town vet—friendly and well known, casual and involved.

He'd become exactly what he'd set out to be. She should have been happy for him. Should have said congratulations or something. Instead, she'd stood there, watching his hands as he calmed the dog, listened to its heartbeat, drew the vial of blood. She'd always liked his hands—they'd been the first thing she noticed when she'd sat beside him in art class in high school. Once, she'd drawn them, hung the sketch over her bed and kept it there until the edges of the paper curled and yellowed.

When they were dating, those same hands had awakened parts of Carolyn she never knew existed. She'd spend her days craving his touch, thinking about him. Even now, a part of her remembered those moments and felt the same simmer of desire.

Not a productive thought at all, especially since she had just agreed to work side by side with the man this week. No thinking about his hands—

Check.

No thinking about the past—

Double check.

No lying to herself that she was definitely thinking about both those things—

Carolyn pled the Fifth on that one. She buckled Emma's booster seat, checked the latch, checked it again, then checked the tension on the seat belt. "You all set in there?"

Emma nodded. "Can I have a snack?"

All Carolyn could picture was Emma choking on a raisin in the back seat. "When we get home, okay?" She climbed into the driver's seat and buckled her seat belt. She drove the couple of miles across town to her parents' house. They still lived in the low-slung ranch house where Carolyn and Sandy had grown up. The white siding was now a soft butter yellow, and the big oak tree that had shaded the front lawn for decades had been lost in a storm two years ago, but everything else appeared to be the same.

Until you got close to the house and saw the paint was fading, the flowers choked by weeds, the garden overgrown. Her parents had gotten old in the time she had been away, as if someone had flipped a switch and fast-forwarded. She'd seen them two Christmases ago when she'd flown them to New York as a Christmas gift, but it seemed like her father had aged twenty years in that time. And her mother—

She was distracted and anxious, hovering over Dad every chance she got.

Bringing a four-year-old and a dog here had seemed like

a great idea when she was hundreds of miles away. Now, Carolyn wasn't so sure. Her plan to have her parents raise Emma was losing steam every day. They were clearly not healthy enough or strong enough to do that.

Which left Carolyn in the same place she'd been five days ago—with a job that was not at all raising-a-kid-friendly and a dog she couldn't control. And a whole lot of expectations left behind by Sandy.

Roscoe bounded out of the car the second Carolyn opened the door, almost toppling her in his rush to freedom. He raced across the yard, trailing his leash behind him. Carolyn cursed, told Emma to stay put, then chased after the dog. Three hundred yards later, Roscoe darted left towards a tree, and Carolyn went right, grabbing the leash loop and wrapping it tight in her hand. "Stay," she said, but Roscoe just jumped up on her, knocking her to the ground and covering her with kisses.

Damned dog.

So maybe working with Matt was a crazy idea, but if it got this dog under control, she'd do crazy. They hadn't dated in ten years—surely enough time had passed that being around him wouldn't affect her. Keep it all business.

Don't think about his hands. Yeah, how well was that plan going so far?

She got Emma out of the car, then went inside, with the not-so-contrite dog padding along beside her. "Don't run off, Emma. Wait for me and Roscoe."

But Emma, much like her beloved puppy, didn't listen. She hurried into the house, dropping a colorful river of coat and hat and toys in her wake. She kept Sandy's sweater clutched to her chest. "Gramma! Can we make cookies?"

At the excitement in Emma's voice, Roscoe broke into a run down the hall. The leash jerked against Carolyn's arm, then slid out of her hand. Roscoe kept on going, undeterred, skidding to a stop beside Emma, thinking he deserved a cookie, too.

Sandy had once told Carolyn that baking cookies together was a favorite activity for Emma and Mom. Unlike Carolyn, Sandy and Bob had visited Marietta often, coming home for all the major holidays and birthdays, and spending two weeks here every summer. Which was part of why Carolyn had been so surprised to be named as Emma's guardian. She barely knew Emma—she could literally count on one hand the number of times she'd seen her—and no matter how hard she tried, Emma stayed reserved and distant from Carolyn, preferring to run to her grandmother for hugs and questions and comfort.

There'd been a few times over the last few days when Emma had teared up, her little body trembling. She'd asked about her mother and father, wondering when they were going to come get her. Mom had taken that question every time, telling Emma that they weren't coming back. Emma didn't seem to grasp that concept yet—or maybe didn't want to—and she always ended up changing the subject and asking for a toy or a book or a TV show. Carolyn knew there would come a moment when Emma finally realized what had happened. She prayed her mother and father were there to help deal with Emma's grief.

Because she sure didn't know how to deal with a little girl. She'd hardly been around kids, and worked in a rushed, stressful environment with a lot of men and a lot of cursing. She had no idea what four-year-olds liked or how to make them happy when their world had just fallen apart.

So she left Emma with Mom a lot, although Carolyn could see the weariness in Mom's face and the toll the days had taken on her, and that only intensified the guilt in Carolyn's gut. Emma brought joy into the house, but she also brought a daily reminder that Sandy would never be here to see her daughter grow up.

"No cookies today." Mom gave Emma a sad smile. "I'm sorry, sweetie. I'm a little tired. Maybe tomorrow?"

"Okay," Emma said, her eyes downcast. She toed at the floor.

"I can make cookies with you, Emma," Carolyn said, putting on a bright smile. That was totally something in Carolyn's wheelhouse. "Whatever kind you want."

"I don't wanna anymore." She clutched the sweater tighter to her chest. "Can I go watch TV?"

"Yes, but only for an hour," Carolyn replied. As she watched Emma head into the living room, her steps slow and sad, Carolyn wondered what else she could have done or said. Sandy would have known. She would have had the perfect words to erase the shadows in Emma's eyes.

Mom turned away, reaching into the cabinet for a mug. Carolyn came up beside her, leaned over and kissed her mother's cheek. "Mom, let me get that. You want some tea?"

Her mother gave her a weak smile. "If it's not too much trouble."

"Trouble is sending out twenty-two chateaubriands at the same time. Making tea is nothing."

"Thank you, honey." Her mother lowered herself into one of the kitchen chairs. She moved a little slower than she used to, took more time to process and think. At sixty-two, Marilyn Hanson still wore the same perfume she'd worn all her life, kept her hair in a blond pageboy that skimmed her chin, and regardless of the plan for the day, dressed in cardigan twinsets with black dress pants.

Her mother used to work as a receptionist at a law office in a nearby town, while her father spent his days building custom furniture in the garage. But ever since Sandy's death, neither of them had worked at all. Carolyn could understand that—there were moments when the grief became this heavy stone wall, and she had to remind herself that she had to keep moving forward. Because Sandy was counting on her.

Carolyn had arrived five days ago, and was staying in the bedroom she'd had as a child, sleeping in her old twin bed, with Emma on the daybed against the opposite wall. Five days and already she was itching to get back to New York, to her own life, to the restaurant.

Five days and she had yet to talk to her parents about Emma. Already almost a week of her two-week leave period was gone. Five days and no plan for how she was going to be a surrogate mom and dog owner. The two things she completely sucked at doing.

Carolyn set a cup of raspberry green tea in front of her mother, then slid into the opposite chair.

"She looks so much like Sandy," her mother whispered even though Emma was out of earshot. "All I keep seeing is your sister, and as much as I love Emma, it breaks my heart all over again."

Carolyn heard the pain in her mother's voice, the shards of grief that hitched on the end of each word. "It still doesn't seem real."

"I don't know if it ever will." Mom's eyes welled, and she turned away, pressing a hand to her nose, and struggling to hold back her tears. Carolyn slid out of her chair and wrapped her arms around her mother. Marilyn held stiff for a moment, then eased into her youngest daughter. She reached around, clutching at Carolyn, while tears dampened their shoulders and grief poured into the space.

After a while, Mom drew back and swiped at her eyes. "I'm sorry, honey. It's still so hard."

"It is for me, too, Mom." With Sandy gone, it felt as if part of Carolyn had been carved away. When they were young, they'd been so close, doing almost everything together. They were only separated by two years, and had stayed just as close after Sandy moved to Wyoming, only a couple hours from Marietta, and Carolyn went to New York. They talked weekly, texted daily. A thousand times since Sandy had died, Carolyn had reached for the phone to call her sister, only to remember she was gone, and the pain hit her all over again.

But no matter how bad it was for Carolyn, it had to be a hundred times harder on her parents. She could see that agony in the lines in her mother's face, the shadows under her father's eyes. A dark cloud hung over the house, invaded every conversation, every glance.

"Your father just stays out in the garage," Mom went on. "I don't know if he is even working on anything. He's out there before I wake up and doesn't come in until I'm asleep." She shook her head. "He's hurting but he's hurting alone."

Carolyn clasped her mother's hand. "He'll come around, Mom. He just needs some time." Marilyn's gaze strayed to the silent garage, where no table saw whined, no wood was being shaped into furniture. "I hope so."

Carolyn hoped so too. She'd barely seen her father since she arrived. Even Emma's presence hadn't been enough to drive Dan back into the house. The light in the garage burned at all hours of the day, and the few times she'd gone out there to talk to her dad, he'd been working and didn't say much.

She remembered the days when her mother would sing

while she did the dishes and her dad would come in from work or the garage, and spin her in his arms. There was laughter and joy in the house, a lightness. That had disappeared since Sandy's death and Carolyn feared it might never return.

"I'm glad I have you and Emma here," Mom said, and a little brightness returned to her words. "And you know you can stay as long as you want. I'm sure it's going to take a while to find a house to rent and a new job and…" Her mother's voice trailed off. "What?"

"About that…" Carolyn drew in a breath. She was going to have to have this conversation someday and delaying it only made things worse. "I know Sandy named me as Emma's guardian but I have a job and a life back in New York. A job that consumes eighty hours a week sometimes, and an apartment smaller than a postage stamp. I can't have a kid and a dog there, Mom."

"Which is why you moved back here."

Carolyn laid her hands flat on the maple kitchen table and waited a beat before she spoke. "I didn't move back. I'm not staying here long term. I'm visiting. In another week, I have to go back to New York."

"But I thought you just said Emma…" Marilyn shook her head. "Carolyn, you're her guardian."

"I can't raise her, Mom. My life, my job—"

"Your father and I are in our sixties, Carolyn. Your father hasn't been the same since his heart attack a few years back, and I'm…I'm exhausted. Taking care of him, grieving the loss of my daughter…" At that, her voice broke, and she let out a long shuddering breath before speaking again. "I love Emma, love her as much as I love you girls, but we're not spring chickens anymore. Keeping up with a four-year-old is tough. And when Emma gets to be a teenager…"

The unspoken words—her parents would be in their seventies, nearly eighty by the time Emma graduated high school. How could Carolyn possibly lay this at their feet? What was she thinking? That wasn't a solution. It wasn't even a partial solution. "I understand. You're right. I guess I'm just not sure how I'm going to do this."

Her mother's hand covered Carolyn's. "One day at a time, honey."

The problem was, Carolyn only had a week to figure out a way to keep her career, her home, and her promise.

Chapter Three

MATT WAS NOT a guy who got nervous. He'd been in stressful situations with life-saving surgeries for a gravely wounded dog hit by a speeding car or a cat with rapidly spreading stomach cancer, but he'd never had that flutter in his stomach or that moment of wondering what the hell he was doing.

But he had all of those feelings in spades today. He paced his house, waiting for Carolyn to arrive with Roscoe, and told himself this was nothing more than one friend doing a favor for another.

Except friends didn't have a history. And memories of making love, seeing her sleep in the soft moonlight streaming in through his bedroom window. She'd only spent the night with him once, when his parents were out of town and she had lied to her parents and told them she was going to a girls' sleepover at a friend's house. That one night had been amazing, and even now, ten years later, he could remember the feel of her in his arms, the way she curled up against him in her sleep, and how her sleepy morning smile nearly undid him.

But those memories were tempered by the one of her breaking his heart. The cold, callous way she had said goodbye, as if their relationship had been nothing more than a blip in her life.

He heard the crunch of gravel and crossed to the door. His own dog, a goofy, patient chocolate Labrador named Harley, trotted along beside Matt. Carolyn got out of her car, opened the back door, but Roscoe had already clambered over the seats and lunged out of the front of the car. Carolyn caught the leash and Roscoe yanked her toward the front door, barking and jerking his way forward.

Matt opened the door and bit back a laugh at the frustration on Carolyn's face. "Who's walking who?"

She scowled. "Don't even ask. That dog chewed up another pair of my heels today. And a sweater. And then he ripped a hole in the screen door trying to go after a squirrel in the backyard."

Matt reached forward, took the leash from Carolyn's hand, and gave Roscoe a slight tug of correction. The dog looked up at him, and settled into place against Matt's hip, his tail wagging with a hard thwap-thwap against Matt's jeans. Harley settled on the floor, letting out a doggie sigh that said he'd seen brash youngsters like this before and he was far too old to put up with such antics.

"Come on in and we'll get right to work with Roscoe," he said to Carolyn. She passed by him, leaving a trail of her fragrance. It wasn't the floral scent of her youth. No, this one was darker, with notes of jasmine and sandalwood, the kind of perfume that whispered about dark nights and tangled sheets. The kind of perfume that made his brain stutter and his heart skip. "Uh…so, you're staying at your parents' house?"

She nodded, shedding her coat. She was wearing a pair of black jeans today—skinny jeans he thought they were called—that outlined every inch of her legs, and a dark green sweater with tempting buttons in the front. "For now. Until I figure out what I'm going to do."

Do with what? He wanted to ask, but reminded himself that they weren't dating anymore. They were barely even friends. He didn't have a right. That didn't stop him from being curious, though.

"I can't stay too long. I left Emma with my mom and she's…not up to watching a four-year-old for too long."

"No problem." He led her down the hall toward the kitchen, with Roscoe trotting happily at his side and Harley bringing up the rear. "Do you want something to drink?"

"Iced tea would be great."

He smiled. "Half unsweetened, half sweet?"

A smile flickered on her face. "You remember."

Instead of answering, he opened the fridge and pulled out two quarts of iced tea. Okay, so maybe when he'd run out to the store this morning and bought them, he'd been hoping she'd be touched that he'd gone the extra mile. But if he told her he'd done that, she'd think he cared, and that door was definitely closed between them. He'd moved on, settled into his life here in Marietta, and the last thing he needed was a complication. And if there was one thing Carolyn Hanson had always been, it was complicated.

"So what are you trying to figure out?" he asked, as he handed her the glass of tea and poured an unsweetened one for himself. So his resolve not to get involved in Carolyn's life again had lasted approximately 8.72 seconds. "Forgive me for asking. It's probably none of my business."

"It's okay." She wrapped her hands around the glass and stared down into the tea. "I haven't really talked to anyone. Everything happened so fast and…" Carolyn sighed and her eyes filled.

Every instinct inside Matt wanted to go to her, to fold her into his arms, and to comfort her. Instead, he leaned against the counter with the two dogs at his feet and waited for her to continue.

"Sandy was in a car accident," Carolyn said finally. "Both her and Bob…I can't even say the words because it still seems so unbelievable, you know?"

Sandy and Bob had died? He remembered Carolyn's sister well. Bubbly, sweet, and friends with about everyone she met. He'd been introduced to Bob one time when he ran into the couple over the holidays a few years ago. Quiet guy, with glasses and a clear affection for his wife. Carolyn's family must be devastated by that double loss—and the orphaned daughter they had left behind. "I'm so sorry, Carolyn. I can't even imagine how hard that has been on your family."

When she lifted her gaze to his, the tears had begun to spill over, and Matt could stand it no longer.

He pushed off from the counter, crossed to her, took the glass from her hands, and set it on the table. Then he pulled Carolyn to her feet and against his chest. She stiffened for a moment, then a sob caught in her throat, and her arms tightened around him. He held her, held her grief with her, while her tears fell. "I'm so sorry, Carolyn. I'm so sorry."

She clung to him for a long time. Then she drew in a breath and stepped out of his embrace, going in an instant from heartbroken to the staid, determined Carolyn he remembered.

"I'm sorry. I shouldn't have done that. I...I just haven't really processed the fact that my sister is gone, and she left me with Emma, and that dog and..." Carolyn threw up her hands. "I don't know what to do with any of that. I'm not a mom. Heck, I can't even keep a dog under control. How am I supposed to raise a kid?"

He didn't have those answers. He had always wanted children, wanted that family life, but both the women he had been in long-term relationships with had wanted other lives. What did that say about him that he picked both Carolyn and Wendy, thinking each one could be a forever kind of woman, only to find out they were on totally different trajectories?

So he retreated to his comfort zone. Animals. "Well, let's start with the dog, and see where that goes. Okay?"

She gave Roscoe a dubious glance. "You really think that dog is going to listen to me?"

"He will, if he realizes it's in his best interests to do so. And if you establish that you're the boss."

She scoffed at that idea. "If I do that, can I fire him as a dog? Because he kinda stinks at the job."

Matt laughed. "It'll be fine. I promise. Let's go outside with Harley and Roscoe and work on some basic obedience."

At the sound of his name, Harley snapped to his feet and crossed to the back door, with Roscoe following along, hapless and joyed just to be going somewhere. Roscoe was a good dog, kinda dumb, kinda sweet, and still young enough to have the energy of a preschool class. Like all dogs, all Roscoe needed was a little structure to get him under control. Matt pulled on the winter coat he kept by the back door, grabbed a small bag from the counter, opened the door, let the dogs out, then held the door for Carolyn.

She brushed past him and once again, he caught a whiff of her perfume. It sent his mind down winding paths that involved his bedroom and a long, lazy night.

Damn.

"Okay. Uh, let's get to work with Roscoe." He had to concentrate on why he was here, not on a woman who had broken his heart a decade ago. He unclipped the leash and the dog took off, circling the yard over and over again, pausing to sniff, then run again. Roscoe was a happy dog, busy and sweet-tempered. Undoubtedly he had been through a lot of changes with the new home and the new master, and that could account for some of his behavior. If Carolyn could establish some leadership, then a lot of the problems with the dog would go away. "Tell him to come."

Carolyn snorted. "Right. Like he's going to listen."

"Use an authoritative voice. Keep the command short, but speak in a tone that says you're the alpha."

"The alpha?"

"Alpha dog." He gave her a grin. "Or in your case, alpha girl."

She laughed. Her breath frosted in the cold air, and her cheeks pinked. She looked younger, cuter. "Is that even a thing?"

"To a dog, it is. A dog wants to obey, wants to please his master. You just need to establish that you're in charge, and he'll fall into place."

Sort of like a teenaged boyfriend who had been so head over heels, he'd been blind to the fundamental differences between them.

Carolyn gave him a dubious look, then bent down, and said to the dog, "Roscoe, come."

The dog ignored her. Started digging a hole to China in the back corner.

"Roscoe, come." She made a face, then raised her voice.

"Roscoe, come!"

Matt moved closer to her. "Women tend to end their sentences with the sound of a question. A dog can hear that, and figures you're an unsure leader. So he ignores you. Try to say it again, but end the command on a flat, stern note."

Carolyn drew in a breath. "Roscoe. *Come*!"

The dog perked his ears up, pivoted toward Carolyn, and hesitated. She repeated the command, and this time, he trotted across the yard like that had been his intention all along. Matt dug in the bag he'd brought outside and handed a dog treat to Carolyn. "Reward him, so he associates doing the right thing with good things happening."

Roscoe stopped before her, tail wagging, nose sniffing the air. "Good boy," Carolyn said, then tossed him the treat. Roscoe caught it midair, swallowed the morsel in one bite, and ran across the yard. They repeated the exercise several times, with Roscoe responding faster each time. In between, Matt gave her some tips for keeping Roscoe under control at home.

"He did it," she said. "He really did it." She turned toward Matt, her face bright and happy, filled with the smile he used to be able to draw in his sleep. "Thank you."

"I didn't do much. You did all the work."

"You gave me hope that maybe I can get this dog under control. And if I can do that…maybe the rest will fall into place, too." She put a hand on his chest, her eyes wide and sincere. "Thank you."

Matt swallowed hard. From the day he met her, whenever Carolyn looked at him that way, he'd been putty in her hands. And right now, with her warm palm against his chest and the dark notes of her perfume drifting in the air, he couldn't quite remember why it wasn't a good idea to get involved with her.

Damn. He still wanted her. Maybe it was the memories whispering through his mind, or the knowledge that they were both adults now, and anything they did together would be that much better, but desire started to simmer inside him all the same.

He shifted a little closer, inches away from her. "I really didn't do anything."

"You did a lot," she said, but the words were a whisper. Her gaze dropped to his mouth, then moved back to his eyes. "Are you going to kiss me?"

"Do you want me to?"

"I think it would be…" her gaze dropped to his lips again and held there for one long, hot second "…an exceedingly bad idea."

"Because…"

"Because we broke up years ago and I'm not staying here and we have to work together and…" She shook her head and backed up, shifting into serious Carolyn as easily as changing her shirt. "And I'm not getting wrapped up in this fairy tale again. We both know that's not real life."

Then she called the dog to her again, snapped on his

leash, and said goodbye to Matt. He watched her go, and cursed himself for getting wrapped up in her spell.

Lesson learned. Again.

NO MATTER HOW much roast beef she ate, or how many mashed potatoes she consumed, the anxious, restless flutter in Carolyn's stomach remained throughout dinner. The encounter with Matt—the moment she had almost kissed him and opened a door she'd shut long ago—had left her shaken. How had they gone from teaching the dog to obey to being inches away? To her wanting nothing more than to kiss him?

She'd sat through a dinner with her parents and Emma that consisted of Emma talking almost nonstop. Dad, still grieving, still broken, stared at his food and pushed it around on his plate. Mom fretted over him, and didn't eat a bite. Carolyn sat between them, at a loss for how to mend the hole torn in the Hanson world.

The entire meal was painful and stiff. After the dishes were cleared and washed, Dad went out to the garage, Mom went into her room to watch television, and a suffocating silence fell over the house. Carolyn set up the baby gates Matt had recommended she get to keep Roscoe in the kitchen—and away from her shoes—then grabbed Emma and got in the car to head downtown.

They pulled up in front of the Marietta ice cream shop with its bright pink and white awning and bistro-style chairs and tables. As soon as Carolyn lifted her out of the booster seat and set her on the sidewalk, Emma started dancing from foot to foot. "Are we getting ice cream? I love ice cream, Aunt Carolyn."

Carolyn could see Sandy in Emma's excitement. She had so much of her mother's personality, along with Sandy's eyes and her smile. The similarities caused an ache in Carolyn's chest. How she wished Sandy was here to indulge in some ice cream and a night in downtown Marietta. "Me too," Carolyn said, forcing a smile to her face and pushing the grief to the back of her mind. "I'd eat it every day if I could."

"You would?" Emma looked up at her. "I wanna eat ice cream every day, too."

Carolyn laughed. "Well, it's not healthy to do that. And if you had it every day, it wouldn't be special anymore, would it?" She opened the door and ushered Emma inside the warm building. It was a nice night for late January in Marietta, with temperatures in the low fifties, a quick anomaly that would be gone in a blink. Not quite ice cream weather but as close as she could get in a Montana winter.

Over the last few days, Emma had had long stretches where she had been quiet and sad, but she usually bounced back pretty easily. Carolyn wondered if maybe Emma hadn't accepted the death of her parents yet, but Carolyn didn't bring it up. What could she say? How could she break this kid's heart? So she bought her toys and took her to the park and out for ice cream.

They stopped at the glass-fronted counter. A rainbow of flavors of ice cream filled the five-gallon tubs inside the freezer chest. A teenage girl with her hair in a ponytail, a ball cap, and a bright pink uniform waited for their order, a ready scoop in her hand.

Carolyn bent down to Emma's level. "So, what flavor is your favorite?"

"Cookie dough!" Emma pointed at the tub filled with vanilla ice cream and chunks of chocolate chip cookie dough.

Something they had in common. It wasn't much, but it was a start, and maybe from there, she could find some way to fill the giant shoes Sandy and Bob had left behind.

"That's my favorite, too," Carolyn said. "Two single scoops of cookie dough, please. And a cup of water." The girl filled their order, Carolyn paid, then she and Emma went over to one of the outdoor tables to eat their melting treats.

"Wait, Emma. Let me clean the seat off—"

But Emma had already scrambled into one of the wrought-iron chairs and wrangled her plastic spoon into the ice cream. Hopefully the usual cold temperatures would have killed off any germs on the table and seat.

"Don't take too big of bites," Carolyn said. "You can get an ice cream headache because it's cold."

Emma smiled when she swallowed, as if the dessert was the best thing she'd ever had. "This is so yummy, Aunt

Carolyn."

"I agree." Carolyn wondered if her face had that same smile when she ate her first bite. She rarely ate ice cream, and when she did, she savored every last morsel. The ice cream from the Creamery was some of the best she'd ever tasted.

"Let me guess. Cookie dough."

Carolyn turned at the sound of Matt's voice. She hadn't even noticed him arrive. His coat was open and she could see he had changed his shirt. Now he had on a faded Springsteen concert T-shirt with his jeans. The T-shirt outlined the muscles in his shoulders, his arms, and the way his waist tapered down to the jeans. Carolyn realized the ice cream wasn't the only thing that made her smile. "Hey, Matt. I can't believe you remember that." And the way she took her iced tea and how to get close enough to drive her wild.

"I remember a lot of things, Carolyn." Before Carolyn could decide what Matt meant by that, he turned to Emma. Harley had wandered over to Emma, nosing at her for a pat on the head. "Seems Harley wants you to share. He's forgetting he's a dog and dogs don't get to eat ice cream."

Emma giggled. "His nose is cold."

"Do you know why?" He bent down beside Emma's seat, and she leaned toward him, eager to hear the secret. "Legend has it that when Noah was on the ark with all the animals, one of the dogs found a hole that was letting water in. If lots of water got in, then the ark could sink. So the dog plugged the hole with his nose, even though the ocean was cold and wet, until Noah could fix it. After that, God gave dogs cold, wet noses to help them cool off when they get too hot."

She patted Harley's nose and giggled again. "Harley would save the ark, too. Harley's a nice dog."

"Best dog I've ever had. I rescued him five years ago, and he's been my buddy ever since."

"Are you gonna get ice cream too?" Emma asked. "Cuz me and Aunt Carolyn have cookie dough and it's our favorite."

"In fact, I *was* stopping in to get an ice cream." He swiveled his attention to Carolyn. "Maybe I could come back and join you after I do?"

She should say no. She should put as much distance between them as possible, keep everything business-only. "Sure. That would be great."

Maybe she'd start doing that tomorrow.

She told herself she'd agreed because this was the happiest she'd seen Emma in a while. Matt seemed to have a natural rapport with her, instead of the stilted conversations Carolyn had with her niece. He made it look so easy, and a part of her envied that.

Matt went inside the shop and emerged a couple minutes later with a dish of strawberry ice cream. He sat down in the third seat. Harley padded over to his master and lay at his feet. "My favorite is strawberry," he told Emma, showing her his dish.

I remember, Carolyn thought. She remembered a lot of

things, too. How he'd loved it when she kissed his neck, how he loved sunrises, and how he liked his coffee dark and strong. She remembered how it felt to kiss him, to be held by him, to lie on a blanket and watch the stars dance over their heads.

"Aunt Carolyn." Emma tugged on Carolyn's sleeve. "You didn't share."

She jerked her attention back to the present. To the conversation going on between Matt and Emma while she'd zoned out. "Uh, share what?"

"Your favorite animal. Dr. Matt's is a giraffe. And my favorite is a elephant. What's yours?"

Well, it sure wasn't dogs. "Um…horses I guess. When I was a little girl, I wanted my parents to buy me a horse for my birthday."

Emma's eyes widened. "Did they?"

"Nope. But that's okay. I go out and ride horses on my day off."

"You still do that?" Matt said softly.

She met his gaze, held it. A memory whispered between them, of a lazy summer afternoon when he'd taken her horseback riding. They had ridden all over the vast Montana landscape surrounding Marietta, stopping by a pond for a picnic lunch, and a sweet moment of privacy under the shade of an oak tree. "Yeah, though my days off are few and far between. I guess you never outgrow some things."

Emma squirmed between them. "I finished my ice

cream. Can I go play with Harley?"

"Sure," Matt said before Carolyn could decide if that was a good idea or not. The moment between them broke.

"Come on, Harley," Emma said. "We're gonna go play!"

"Put your trash away first," Carolyn said. She nodded toward a metal can a few feet away. The three of them tossed their empty containers inside it, then Carolyn put a halting hand on Emma's shoulder. "Wait, Emma. Don't move yet."

Carolyn wet an extra napkin with her water, then scrubbed the sticky ice cream from Emma's hands. Emma twisted and turned, anxious to be gone. "Let me straighten your coat and—"

"I wanna go play, Aunt Carolyn!"

"She's just going to get messy in the park," Matt said. "It'll be fine."

"I think I should—"

Matt covered her hand with his. "It'll be fine. Kids get messy. Just relax, Carolyn."

She couldn't tell him that relaxing was the one thing she had yet to do since she arrived in Marietta. Every time Emma went anywhere or did anything, Carolyn worried. "I just want to make sure she's safe and healthy."

The unspoken words—*because I can't lose her, too, and I can't let Sandy down.*

"It'll be fine. Come on, let's get to the park before it's dark. Crawford Park is really close by." They walked down the street to the large park: a lush, green space filled with a playground for kids, benches for enjoying the day, and trees older than the town itself. The sun had begun to go down while they were eating their ice cream, casting the park in hues of purple and dark pink.

Emma broke into a run, barreling across the grassy space. Harley let out a bark and galloped after her. "Wait, Emma, don't—"

"She'll be fine," Matt said again.

"But the dog—"

"Harley's good with kids. He knows better than to jump on them, and he's pretty protective. Let her run off some energy. She'll sleep better tonight."

They fell into an easy stroll, trailing the dog and Emma. Carolyn's heart hammered with worry and a thousand potential worries about germs and falls and anything that could go wrong with a kid in a park with an energetic dog.

"Emma sleeping tonight would be a godsend," Carolyn said. "It seems like she has extra energy just before she's supposed to go to bed."

Matt chuckled. "I bet it's been tough stepping into Sandy's shoes."

Carolyn knew she was barely functioning as Emma's mom. Handing her off to Gramma for storytime at night wasn't the same as being there to answer the hard questions, or figuring out a life that would accommodate both raising a child and having a career. Plenty of women did that every day, so surely there was a way Carolyn could make it work, too.

"I'm not a mom. I'm not maternal," Carolyn said. "Ask me to whip up a seven-course meal for thirty people, and I'm in my element. But when it comes to grieving four-year-old girls, I have no idea what to do. I worry about everything—if she's wearing a sweater, if she ate her vegetables, if she slept enough, if she's…" She cursed. "Heading for the sandpit. Isn't that a box full of germs?"

"Number one, kids are resilient. Emma's tougher than you give her credit for. They're designed to get a little rough and tumble and dirty, and be totally okay."

Emma sat on the bench that ringed the sandpit. A panting Harley sat down beside her. Emma draped her arm around the Lab and gave him a big hug, the two of them with their heads together, shadowed by the dim light of dusk. If she'd been a painter, Carolyn would have captured that tender moment on canvas.

"I just don't want to let Sandy down," Carolyn said. "I still have no idea how I'm going to raise Emma. In a week, I'm going back to New York, back to my job."

"Your mom told me you're a chef at a fancy restaurant in Manhattan."

"Sous chef. Up for promotion to head chef. Which won't happen if I can't put in the hours the restaurant needs." She sighed. "I don't see how I'm going to balance it all."

"You're strong and smart, Carolyn. I'm sure you'll figure something out."

She scoffed. He had no idea the hours she worked, the days when she got to bed in the wee hours of the morning, grabbed a few hours of sleep, then started all over again. That was no way to raise a child—Emma would spend more time with nannies and babysitters than anyone else. "You have more faith than I do."

"I know you pretty well, remember?" He gestured toward one of the benches.

She nodded, and they took a seat. The bench was short, and their hips nearly touched. Carolyn wasn't sure if she liked that or not. Harley and Emma ran circles around the grassy expanse before them, Emma's laughter carrying on the slight breeze.

"Remember the prom planning committee?" Matt said. "At the last minute, the DJ canceled and the hall shut its doors. Within twenty-four hours, you had found a new location, a new DJ, and managed to bring the cost down by ten bucks a ticket."

"That really wasn't a big deal. A few phone calls."

"It was a big deal to the entire senior class." He tore the end off a long blade of grass and tossed it at the ground. "You sure impressed me. I remember thinking: this girl is way out of my league."

"Me? I thought you were ten notches above me in the social stratosphere." She braced her hands on the edge of the bench, pretending not to notice how the edge of her palm brushed his leg. "Captain of the football team, voted best smile, the one guy every girl in school wanted to date."

"Wait. *Every* girl in school? Was there some tweet about that I missed?"

She gave him a light slug in the arm. "You were dating me, you big idiot. I wasn't going to tell you about the other girls who were interested."

A smirk filled his face. "Are you saying you were jealous?"

"It was high school. Everyone was immature then."

"You didn't answer the question, Carolyn."

Because doing that would mean admitting she had cared. That it still bothered her a little bit. That a part of her wondered how a guy as good-looking as Matt was still single.

Instead of saying any of that, she rolled her eyes and played it off as a joke. "I was what, seventeen, eighteen? All girls are insecure at that age."

"Not you," he said. "Out of everyone I knew, you seemed like you really had yourself together. You knew what you wanted to be, how you were going to get there…and where you wanted to live."

She heard notes of hurt in the last few words. Ten years ago, she had stood with Matt in the high school parking lot, and told him she was leaving town and never coming back. He'd been slack-jawed, stunned. Angry.

He hadn't heard the fear in her voice, the part of her waffling about her decision. The part that secretly wanted Matt to beg her to stay, or beg her to take him with her. He'd done neither. He'd let her go with just a cold, *Well, I guess that's it.* She'd hurried out of the parking lot before he could see her tears.

But now she thought of what she'd just said. How everyone was a little immature in high school. Maybe Matt had been too, unable to voice the emotions he was feeling, or reacting from his gut instead of his heart. Would it really hurt to admit the truth now? After all, it had been ten years. Maybe telling him why she had left so abruptly would give him some closure. Give both of them a little.

"If I told you while we were dating, we would have broken up," she said softly. "And I didn't want that."

"Why not?"

Because I really liked you. Because I kept hoping we'd find a way to compromise. Because I was young and foolish and running around with stars in my eyes.

"I should get Emma home," Carolyn said as she got to her feet. "It's past her bedtime."

"Yeah. I've stayed here too long, too." Matt called Harley to his side, waved goodbye to Emma, then headed in the opposite direction. Just like ten years ago, he let the subject go. Let her go.

For a moment, Carolyn watched him leave, then she turned away, focusing on her niece. Everything she needed to worry about right now was in this four-year-old bundle of energy. Dwelling in the past was the kind of foolish thing starry-eyed teenage girls did.

Chapter Four

MATT MADE IT through his workday in record time. There were no emergencies, nothing beyond routine physicals and shots. He almost wished for something exciting, because his mind wandered during the mundane.

Wandered to thoughts of Carolyn. To the past. To the day she'd broken his heart, and the day she'd walked back into his life.

Like he had ten years ago, he'd reacted to her admission the same way—by steeling his heart and walking away. He'd already been hurt deeply by Carolyn once. He didn't want to make it a second time.

She was still beautiful, still had a way of smiling at him that made his heart race. And damn it all, he still wanted to kiss her. Even if that would be a colossal mistake.

Sheryl poked her head into his office. "All done for the day. Do you need me for anything else?"

"Nope, I'm good."

"Don't forget the Bake-Off is this weekend. Have you figured out what you're going to fake-bake?"

He chuckled. "I'm going to really bake. I have a baking tutor." Which sent his mind down all kinds of *Hot for Teacher* paths.

And put him, he realized, right back in the middle of the same quandary. Stay away from the woman who had broken his heart and surely would again if he did something about the desire he still felt for her—or try to keep it all business, a little dog training for a little baking?

Yeah, considering how close he'd come to kissing her the other day, that all-business thing was already a lost cause.

Sheryl laughed. "A baking tutor? Oh, I am totally buying a ticket to the Bake-Off. I have got to see this. I'll sit in the back, in case you need a heckler."

"Hey, this is for a good cause." He wagged his pen at her. "Not an opportunity to harass the guy who signs your paycheck."

"Sure, boss. Whatever you say." Sheryl laughed, then waved goodbye. A few minutes later, Matt finished typing up the last of his notes, and closed up the office for the day. He drove through Marietta, marveling at how the town had maintained its quaint setting, even as new businesses came and went, setting up shop beside places that had been there for generations. He'd always loved this town, the warm people who had become good friends over the years. He couldn't imagine leaving it for the hustle and anonymity of a place like New York City.

What about that had appealed to Carolyn? He'd always

wondered why she'd chosen Manhattan over Marietta. What had she found there—

And *who* had she found there?

That was the one question he had yet to ask her—was she dating anyone? She didn't have a ring on her finger, so if she was, the relationship wasn't serious.

Was he considering dating her again? That would be insane—she had told him she was only here for one more week, before she went back to New York. He already knew how this story would end. Only a fool read the same unhappy book twice.

Except a part of him was still anticipating seeing her tonight, even if it wasn't a date.

He went home, let Harley out, showered and changed. A little after six, his doorbell rang. He made a visual sweep of his kitchen, straightened his shirt, smoothed his hair, as nervous as he'd been the first time he'd asked Carolyn out. His hair had been longer then, his body thinner, and his voice a pitch higher. He'd stood beside her table at the end of art class, screwed up his courage, and asked if she wanted to go see the latest Harry Potter movie.

He didn't remember a single line from the movie, couldn't recall one frame of the picture. But he did remember how he had put his arm around Carolyn a few minutes in, and she had curled against him in the darkened theater, and sealed his heart to hers.

He'd loved how smart she was, how efficient. How the

things she created in art were always a bit to the left of everyone else's. When they had to draw a shoe, she drew the tattered sole and open toe of a lost boot while everyone else was drawing Nike sneakers. For a still life, she had drawn melting ice cubes in a stack. They'd looked so real, Matt half expected them to puddle on the floor. His own sketch of a couple bananas and a pineapple paled in comparison.

And he'd loved the way she loved him—or at least he'd thought she'd loved him. She would sneak notes into his books when he wasn't looking, or bake him brownies or snuggle into his sweatshirt, leaving the fresh scent of her perfume behind when he put it over his head later. Even though he had dated since, and even married Wendy, he'd never felt quite the same as he had in high school—like he lived somewhere up in the clouds.

Infatuation, his mind reminded him. The silly infatuation of a teenager. He was a grown-up now and those crazy days were behind him.

He pulled open the door. "Hey, Carolyn." Aiming for nonchalant, as if he hadn't just been thinking about her.

"Hey, Matt." She placed a heavy white and silver machine in his hands, then picked up a grocery bag by her feet. "Bring that in please, and we'll get started."

All business, no flirting. He told himself that was what he wanted. She was leaving soon, and this was simply a temporary alliance. Dog training for baking training. And definitely no kissing in the middle of either.

He set the machine on his kitchen counter. "That thing weighs a ton. What is it?"

"A mixer. The best one ever, if you ask me."

To Matt, the white appliance looked sturdy enough to blend cement. Of course, this was coming from the guy who only owned a couple of pans and mostly ate off of paper plates. "Because I need all the help I can get?"

She laughed. He'd always liked her laugh, the way it sounded like wind chimes in a light breeze. "From what I remember about your culinary skills, you're going to need a *miracle*."

"I'd take offense, but I have a sneaking suspicion you're right." He leaned against the counter and watched while Carolyn unloaded the groceries, setting them up in order, labels facing front. "You're still a little OCD."

"I just like things neat and tidy. And in a busy kitchen, having everything where you expect it is essential." She stepped back, assessed the ingredients, then gestured toward Matt. "Okay, let's get baking. Today, we're making peanut butter cookies. They're simple, and similar to what we'll be making for the Bake-Off, but a little easier. Later this week, we'll tackle our actual Bake-Off recipe. So this will give you a good taste—"

"No pun intended."

She laughed. "Okay, maybe that was the wrong term. But this will let you get a sample of the cookie-making process. We're not doing anything too complicated, but hopefully something tasty. First things first—start with the recipe."

Later this week. That meant they'd have another one of these tutoring sessions. Was it wrong to be glad for that? To already be anticipating it?

Maybe not wrong, but not smart. Focus, he told himself. Focus.

He glanced over at the handwritten sheet she'd laid beside the mixer. Like the ingredients, Carolyn's recipe was neatly printed, with bulleted instructions. First step, preheat the oven to 350 degrees. "Uh…how do I preheat?"

Laughter burst from her and she shook her head. "Okay, I take it back. I don't know if a miracle is going to be enough. All right, let's go back a few steps to the basics." She leaned over the oven and pointed at the keypad. Her shirt edged up above her waist, exposing a thin strip of peach skin.

He wanted to put his hands on her waist, to feel her warmth beneath him. To hear her whisper his name—

Okay, not productive. At all. He was supposed to be preheating the oven, not his libido.

"So just set this at 350," Carolyn was saying, "and when the oven is ready, it will beep. In the meantime, we'll start mixing the ingredients."

"Preheat. Got it." He pressed the button she indicated, then stepped back. "What's next?"

"Hold up, cowboy." She picked up the handwritten sheet and gave it to him.

Cowboy. The word sent Matt's attention down a path that involved a late night, a big bed, and a whole lot of time with Carolyn.

Grade for focusing—a D, and only if he was grading himself on a bell curve.

"Read the recipe," she said, and his attention swiveled back to what they were doing. "Read it all the way to the end, so you aren't taken by surprise halfway through. Make sure you have all the ingredients, and *then* you can start baking."

Matt scanned the recipe for peanut butter cookies. It seemed pretty easy, and clear-cut. Even for someone like him with limited kitchen skills. "Okay, it says to first mix the butter, brown sugar, and white sugar until creamy and smooth."

When he reached for the butter, Carolyn put a hand on his arm. The light touch sent a shiver of electricity through his veins. "First, make sure you have all the things you need. Then start measuring."

He reread the recipe, then glanced at the items on the countertop. "Wait, there's no peanut butter." He shot her a grin. "Was that a test?"

"Yup." She laughed.

He shifted closer to her. He loved to make her smile, loved to hear her laugh. The sound added a brightness to his kitchen, to his home. "And did I pass?"

"Depends…" she said, her gaze dropping to his mouth

for a second, "on how the cookies turn out."

He watched the words form on her lips, and realized it had been a long, long time since he'd wanted to kiss someone as much as he wanted to kiss Carolyn right now. She had her hair up in a clip, exposing that long, graceful neck he loved so much. Desire thudded in his veins, urging him to close the gap between them to inches. "I bet they're going to be sweet and warm and once you have one, you're going to want another."

She arched a brow. "Pretty confident in yourself, aren't you?"

"I have experience."

"In baking? I thought you said—"

"I wasn't talking about cookies, Carolyn." The words hung in the heated air between them for a long moment before she spoke.

"Oh." Her gaze dropped to his mouth again and when she spoke, her voice was softer, darker. "*Oh.*"

She didn't move away. She didn't back up. Her gaze locked with his, and a slight smile flickered on her face. He leaned in closer, drawn by those eyes, that perfume, and all the history that told him how sweet kissing Carolyn would be.

His lips met hers, slow, tentative at first, tasting and teasing. Her palm pressed against his chest. Heat surged inside him. He deepened the kiss when she opened against him, his tongue sweeping in against hers. He put his hands on her waist, fingers sliding against that bare expanse of skin. Carolyn let out a soft mew, and arched toward him.

Good Lord, he had missed her. Missed the way she tasted, the way she smelled, the way her skin felt beneath his. A part of him wanted to take her into his bedroom, and make love to her until the sun began to peek above the horizon. Instead, he drew back, releasing her, while the rest of his body protested.

Where was he going to go with this? Better to end the kiss now, while he still had a leash on the desire inside him.

"What...what are we doing?" she asked, the words a bit breathless.

"Taking a short stroll down memory lane." No more. No dating her or sleeping with her or getting his heart wrapped up in her again. Uh-huh. And so far his record for not getting involved with Carolyn was worse than the batting average of the Mets.

She cleared her throat and turned away. "The, uh, butter is already softened, so all you, uh, have to do is measure the sugars and add them with the sticks of butter."

Changing the subject to something neutral. Back to business as usual, as if the kiss had never happened. He should have been glad. Instead, he was disappointed. He dragged his mind back to the recipe. "I thought I still needed peanut butter."

"Oh, yeah, I uh, put it in my purse. To see if you'd notice it was missing." She crossed to the table, dug in her bag, and pulled out the jar. "So, we have everything and we can get to work."

Still not a word about the kiss. About whether she wanted to stroll down memory lane with him. Matt told himself to be relieved. Getting involved with Carolyn—especially when he knew how this would end—was insane.

The kind of crazy thing he would have done when he was younger, brasher, less aware of what the future held. Ten years later, he knew the only thing he should be anticipating was the fresh-baked cookies.

CAROLYN HOPED TO God that Matt wouldn't notice she was trembling when she handed him the measuring cups. That kiss…

Had been spectacular. It was as if they'd never been apart. His lips had moved across hers with the knowledge of a man who knew his history. When he'd told her he remembered more than just the way she took her iced tea or her favorite ice cream flavor, he wasn't kidding.

Her body still simmered from his touch, and she could swear where he'd held her waist was ten degrees warmer than the rest of her. She kept glancing over at him as he turned on the mixer, waited for the butter and sugars to cream together, then followed her instructions for adding the eggs one at a time.

Baking with him also put her attention on his hands, which left her distracted and flustered and thinking about how it felt when he touched her. Damn.

"Do I really have to break them into this bowl first?" Matt asked, and it took her a second to realize he was talking about the eggs. "Seems like an extra step and extra dishes."

"Considering you're not exactly an egg-breaking pro—" she fished out a piece of shell "—this is better than getting shells in your cookie dough."

He finished breaking the eggs into the small bowl, tipped them into the mixture, then watched as they disappeared with the mixer's revolutions. "Okay, what's next? Wait. Don't tell me." He thought for a second. "One cup of peanut butter."

"Exactly." She picked up a skinny spatula and used it to scoop the gooey peanut butter into the measuring cup. She shifted closer to Matt, acutely aware of the heat from his body, the close proximity of his chest, his hips, his hands. She slid the peanut butter into the mixer and went to reach for the flour when Matt stopped her.

"You have peanut butter on the back of your hand." He caught her hand with his, and held it up. "Wouldn't want that getting into the flour. It could mess everything up."

Her heart skipped a beat. God, she was already thinking about kissing him again. Fantasizing about much, much more. "That would...that would, ah, definitely be bad."

"I agree. We should make sure that doesn't happen." He

raised her hand to his mouth, and kissed the dollop of peanut butter off. She inhaled, and tried not to melt right there on the spot. The movement lasted only a second, but her body reacted in a flash of heat and want. For a second, she wanted to slather her body in peanut butter and see where his mouth went next.

"I...I think you got it all," she said and tugged her hand out of his. This wasn't productive, nor was it wise. She was leaving town in a few days, and she already knew where a relationship with Matt would lead. They'd circle back around to the white picket fence life talk, and she'd break his heart all over again.

The second time, she was sure it would hurt twice as much. Especially for her.

"Sorry." Matt stepped back. "Peanut butter is one of my favorite foods."

"I remember," she whispered. For a second, neither of them moved, still caught in that tangle between desire and common sense. She cleared her throat and got back into her comfort zone—the organized safety of a recipe. "Okay, so now we have to sift together the dry—"

Matt arched a brow. "Sift?"

She picked up her flour sifter, and held it out to him. It was like a tiny wall between them. "Sift."

He muttered something about extra steps and extra dish-es again, but did as she said, measuring the dry ingredients into the metal container, then pulling the handle, sending cloud-light flour drifting into a bowl. "This is crazy. I can't use this thing during the Bake-Off. It'll take forever."

She laughed. "We can pre-sift the dry ingredients so they're ready to mix that day. I read the rules, and some prep work is allowed."

"There are rules?"

She propped her fists on her hips. "You really are totally unprepared for this, aren't you?"

"I'm a card-carrying, pizza-ordering bachelor; of course I'm not prepared for this."

She handed him the salt and watched as he added it on top of the flour. "Why?"

"Why what?"

"Why..." She measured out the baking soda and dumped it into the sifter. "Why are you still a bachelor?"

Loaded question of the day. Where had that come from? It wasn't like she was still interested in him—okay, so maybe her reaction to that kiss and his very sexy peanut butter removal said otherwise—but still, they were ancient history.

He kept on sifting, and for a while, the only sound in the kitchen was the soft ch-ch of the sifter sliding in and out. "I did get married. Two years ago."

"Really?" She gestured toward the mixer, because if she pretended to be more interested in the cookie dough than his answer, maybe he wouldn't see how much it stunned her— and hurt a little—that he'd been married to someone else. She hadn't expected Matt to stay a monk after they broke up, of course, but thinking of him falling in love with another woman gave her pause. "Add the dry ingredients gradually while the mixer is running."

"That sounds like a recipe for trouble."

She laughed. "Just keep the mixer on a low speed. Unless you want to flour bomb your kitchen."

"That was my plan for next week." He grinned, then did as she said. He watched the arm of the mixer revolve, tipping the dry ingredients in a little at a time.

"So…what happened?" Carolyn asked, cursing herself for showing curiosity. She blamed it all on that kiss and their close proximity. "Because I don't see a wife in your kitchen now."

He kept on watching the mixture of dry ingredients tumble into the metal bowl and get caught in the constant swirl of the blade. "After we got married, Wendy decided she didn't want the same future I did, and we broke up."

"Sounds like a common story." She shook her head. She really was a glutton for punishment, wasn't she? Retreading old, painful history? Why did she care so much? "Sorry."

"It's okay. You'd think I would have learned to have these conversations earlier in the relationship." His smile disappeared almost as fast as it appeared.

Ten years had passed, but the hurt still lingered in his voice. Carolyn had thought about the day she left a hundred times in the years since, and knew she had taken the coward's way out. Break his heart and get out of town, so she didn't have to see Matt and face that she had let a good man go. A good man who didn't want to travel the same path as she did. A good man who wanted a different life from her. She'd told herself it was easier, quicker, less painful.

But she had lied.

"I'm really sorry about what happened between us that day," Carolyn said. She put her back to the counter and braced her hands on the edge. "I shouldn't have just broken up with you and run out of town. I did it because I was afraid…"

"Afraid of what?"

She hesitated for a long time. Why had she started this conversation? Opening up the past was like opening Pandora's box. She should know enough to leave well enough alone. It had to be being back in this town, surrounded by all these reminders of the life she used to have. And that stroll down memory lane, as Matt had called their kiss. It had brought all the old feelings to the surface, paired them with years-old regrets. "I was afraid…if I stayed in town I'd change my mind."

"Really?" He turned off the mixer and pivoted toward her. His brown eyes softened with surprise. "And would that have been such a bad thing?"

She shook her head. What-ifs were for dreamers. Carolyn was practical, realistic. She thought of the last conversation she'd had with her grandfather before he died. The grandfather who had taught her to cook, the grandfather who had seemed to understand her, to know what drove Carolyn. *Don't get stuck in this little town and leave your dreams behind you,* he'd said. *When you're young, you have the freedom to run after what you want. So run, Carolyn, run before you end up...here.*

Here meaning the small town where her grandfather had ended up working in an automotive repair shop for forty years instead of pursuing the cooking dream he loved. Here where he'd ended up married at nineteen, saddled with three children before he was twenty-three, and caught in that need to make money and support his family instead of taking a chance on chasing his dream of being a chef.

That was what Carolyn hadn't wanted. To marry Matt after high school, or even after college, and end up in Marietta, maybe working as an assistant like her mother had, and never knowing what she might have found if she left.

"I would have never been happy here, Matt," she said, because that was simpler than putting all the rest into words.

"In this town. With me."

Everything circled back to Marietta. The small-town life Carolyn had felt suffocated by was the very life Matt loved. "We should bake the cookies," she said instead of answering him. "It's getting late."

And the longer she stayed here, in this warm, cozy kitchen next to the man she used to love, the closer she came to the very past she had left behind ten years ago.

Chapter Five

MATT SAT AT his kitchen table, drinking coffee and eating peanut butter cookies while Harley snoozed in the bright Sunday morning sun streaming in through the windows. He heard a familiar double knock at the back door, called out, "It's open," and went back to his cookies. They were damned good cookies, if he said so himself.

His brother Scott strode into the kitchen, wearing a thick running jacket, long running pants, and sneakers. Taller, even though he was a year younger, Scott had always had a lanky build, leaner than Matt. It suited him for his job as a roofer, because he could scramble up a ladder faster than most people could set one against the house. "You ready?"

"Almost." Matt ate the last bite of cookie and got to his feet.

Scott chuckled. "You're seriously going to run five miles on a breakfast of cookies?"

"Hey, they're peanut butter. That means there's protein in them." And sugar, and butter, but he wasn't going to mention that. After they'd finished baking, Carolyn had left most of the batch with him, taking just a handful to bring home to Emma.

Every time he caught the scent of peanut butter or glimpsed the platter on his table, he thought of her. Hell, he'd tossed and turned most of the night, thinking of her. About kissing her, tasting her, wanting her. And how she had thrown up that wall between them all over again.

Still, she had surprised him when she said she had left town in a rush because she was afraid she'd change her mind. All these years, he'd painted Carolyn as the callous one, breaking his heart and embarking on her new life without a thought for what she'd left behind in Marietta. When it turned out, like anything, there were layers and complications to the past.

Scott plucked a cookie from the plate on the table and took a bite. "These are good. Who made them?"

"Me."

Scott coughed, and laughed, almost choking on his bite. "Right. I've seen you burn water. You can barely make yourself a bowl of cereal in the morning."

Which was why he was eating cookies for breakfast. He might have learned one recipe, but that didn't turn him into Mario Batali overnight. Though he did hope there were more baking lessons in the future. Just for the cookies...or at least that's what he told himself. "I'm practicing for the Bake-Off. I signed up to compete on the first day, and then realized I was actually going to have to bake, so I got...a baking tutor."

Scott arched a brow. "A baking *tutor*? Who the hell does that in Marietta?"

"Carolyn Hanson."

Both brows arched now, Scott let out a low whistle. "Carolyn Hanson, as in your old girlfriend? What's she doing back in town?"

Now he was sorry he had mentioned her name. He knew his younger brother and knew there was a waterfall of questions coming. A part of him wanted to talk about Carolyn, though, if only to give voice to the turmoil churning in his gut. Maybe then he could stop thinking about her. "Her sister and her sister's husband Bob were killed in a car accident," Matt said. "Carolyn has custody of Sandy's four-year-old daughter. She's here for a couple weeks while she figures out what to do." And then she was leaving town again, just as she had ten years ago. He seemed to keep forgetting that.

"Wow, that's awful about Sandy. I didn't know her well because she was a few years older than me, but she always seemed nice." Scott shook his head. "And now Carolyn is tutoring you because…?"

Matt laced up his running shoes, grabbed Harley's leash, and led Scott outside. The icy winter air hit him like a wall. It hadn't snowed in a while, so winter in Marietta right now consisted of cold and more cold. Soon as they got their run underway, Matt knew he'd be warm enough to want to unzip his jacket, but for now, it was bitterly cold. "Because I'm helping her with some dog training. Sandy also left behind a rambunctious mutt. Good dog, but needs some discipline."

"Trading favors, huh?" Scott fell into place beside Matt as they started with a light jog. Their breaths formed twin bursts of clouds in the brisk morning. "Trading anything else?"

This was the part of the run where everything inside of Matt wanted to retreat to the warmth of his house. He knew if he stuck with it, though, his body would warm and sink into a rhythm and the agony of starting in the bitter January cold would ease. "She's leaving town in a week."

"Which doesn't answer my question."

Because answering Scott's question would mean admitting that except for a couple of kisses, Matt hadn't gotten close to Carolyn. Not that he hadn't thought about it once or twice. Or a hundred times. "Getting involved with her would be crazy. Been there, did that, learned my lesson."

"Which still doesn't answer my question." Scott swung in front of Matt and began to run backward. "And I think you're avoiding the answer because you two have been doing—"

"We have not." Matt ducked to the left, putting his brother and his brother's knowing grin behind him. "I kissed her, but it was nothing."

"Nothing? Really?"

Matt had never been good at lying, and even worse at lying to his brother. Everything between him and Carolyn was more than nothing. But what it was...he didn't know yet. Wasn't sure if he should even figure it out. "You know, it's going to be a long five miles if you keep throwing out questions like that."

Scott grinned again. "That's what I'm hoping for."

CAROLYN WOKE UP before Emma on Sunday morning. She padded down to the kitchen, but it was empty and quiet, no coffee brewing. Her mother must still be in bed, which didn't surprise Carolyn, but did sadden her. Normally, her mother rose early, getting in a morning walk before church or working in the garden. But since Sandy had died...

Nothing was the same. And probably never would be. The best they could all do was move forward. Carolyn put on a pot of coffee, then noticed the light on in the garage.

She poured two cups, then slipped outside and across the walk to the garage. Roscoe nudged past her, and started sniffing around the fenced yard. It had rained overnight, and the yard was soft, spongy, the air crisp and fresh.

The side garage door was ajar, letting in the cold winter air. "Hey, Dad," she said, entering the workshop and holding out one of the mugs. "I brought you some coffee."

"Thanks." Her father took the cup and sat back on a

stool. He had aged a lot in the last few years, his once salt and pepper hair gone completely white. Shadows dusted the space under his eyes and lines filled his face.

Carolyn ran a hand down the smooth surface of the end table her father was working on. A dark maple, with an inlay of lighter oak, and elaborately turned legs that must have taken hours on the lathe. "This is gorgeous, Dad. Is it an order? Or for the house?"

"I was making it for…" His voice trailed off and the words choked in his throat. Tears filled his eyes and he shook his head. "It's not done yet."

In an instant, Carolyn regretted mentioning the table because she knew, without her father saying a word, who the table was meant for. Carolyn remembered her sister mentioning that she had asked Dad to build some new pieces for their living room. She'd been so excited, talking about how nice it was to talk with Dad and work out the plans. Now the house was going to be sold, and the furniture would remain in this garage. And Sandy would never see the craftsmanship and love that had gone into a simple piece of furniture.

"I'm sorry, Dad," Carolyn said. She stepped back from the piece and leaned against the workbench. She didn't know what else to say, how else to make it right. Getting close to people had been Sandy's skill, not hers. "Mom is worried about you."

"Yeah, I know."

"She told me you aren't talking to her." Carolyn wrapped both hands around her coffee. Maybe if she could at least get her parents talking to each other again, she could go back to New York and not have this constant worry in her gut. She worried about Emma, worried about where they were going to live, worried about how she was going to make it all work out. Maybe if she could get one corner of her life—and her family—straightened out, then the rest would fall into place. "She needs you too, Dad."

He put his coffee on top of his toolbox, then picked up a sanding block and started running it down a short piece of wood sitting on the bench. "I have work to do."

Except the piece of wood he was working on looked more like scrap lumber to Carolyn than anything else. And his movements lacked any real strength, more of a skim than a sand. "Emma and I are going to the park with Roscoe this morning," Carolyn said. "Do you want to come with us?"

"Maybe another time." Dad had turned away, and the hunch of his shoulders already said the conversation was over. Carolyn waited a moment more—the only sound coming from the swish-scratch of the sandpaper—then she took her coffee and went back inside. She didn't know what else to say, or how to make it better.

Roscoe caught up to her as she reached the back door, squeezing past her legs to be the first inside. Before she could tell him to sit or stay, he was off, circling the kitchen with muddy paws, then jumping on the bar stools and putting his paws on the counter. "Roscoe, no!"

"He likes to run, Aunt Carolyn." A sleepy Emma stood in the doorway, still wearing her pink flannel nightgown and clutching her mother's sweater.

"That he does. And now the entire kitchen knows that, too." She sighed, then grabbed a rag from the bucket under the kitchen sink and wet it. She scooped some dog food into Roscoe's bowl—the only way to get that dog to stay in the same spot for more than ten seconds. While Roscoe ate, Carolyn cleaned up the mud.

Emma climbed on top of one of the bar stools. She watched her aunt finish tidying up the kitchen, then pour a bowl of Cheerios and set them on the counter. "I don't want Cheerios."

"That's okay. I can make you some eggs." Carolyn gave Emma a smile. "I make a really great omelet if you want that instead."

Emma shook her head. "I don't want eggs."

"Toast with peanut butter?" Maybe simpler was better. Carolyn realized she had no idea what Emma's favorite breakfast was, what she was allergic to, what her favorite color was. Sandy had been the one to keep track of the details. Carolyn had operated on autopilot, pouring Cheerios because that was what she and her sister had sat here and ate almost every morning when they were kids.

"I don't want toast. I'm not hungry." Emma drew the sweater closer to her chest, burrowing her face in the wool, as if she could still catch Sandy's scent in those fibers.

"Okay. Maybe in a little while." While Carolyn cleaned, Emma sat on the stool, quiet. Pensive.

"When are we going home to see my mommy?"

The soft-spoken question seemed to echo. Carolyn stopped mid-movement, running water soaking the rag, her hands. The water was cold, but Carolyn barely felt the temperature. What was she supposed to say? How was she supposed to answer Emma? Every time, Carolyn had defaulted to her mother, letting Grandma take those tough questions. But this time, it was just her and Emma and Roscoe, and the dog wasn't talking.

Carolyn turned off the water and pivoted toward her niece. "We can't do that, honey."

"I wanna go home. I wanna be at my house." Emma's lower lip trembled, and her eyes filled. She clutched the sweater like a lifeline.

"Your mom and dad aren't there anymore, Emma," Carolyn said.

"Where did they go?"

Oh, God, this was a question way above Carolyn's pay grade. She didn't have Sandy's tender touch, her soft words. Carolyn was used to barking orders at the cooks in the kitchen, not dancing around delicate subjects with a preschooler. Hell, Carolyn had barely even processed Sandy's death herself—how was she supposed to do that with Emma?

"Emma, we're going to the park today, remember?"

Maybe a change of subject would help shift Emma's attention. Carolyn forced brightness into her voice. "Do you want to—"

"I don't wanna go to the park! I wanna go home, Aunt Carolyn! I wanna see my mommy. I wanna go home!" With every word, Emma's voice rose. Roscoe scooted under the table, his tail flat and his head on his paws. Carolyn stood there, helpless, unsure what to do.

"I wanna go home! I wanna go now!"

Her mother came into the kitchen, already dressed for the day, even though the chances of her leaving the house were nonexistent. "What's all the—" She cut off the sentence when she saw Emma's face. Marilyn leaned down and put a hand on Emma's shoulder. "What's the matter, honey?"

"I wanna go home, Grandma." Emma's voice softened and cracked, and the tears in her eyes brimmed and began to fall.

Mom looked at Carolyn. Carolyn shook her head. Her throat closed, the right words lost somewhere inside her. Once again, she questioned her sister's sanity in naming her as Emma's guardian. "I, uh, have to get ready for the trip to the park. Mom, can you...?"

Carolyn was halfway out of the kitchen when her mother caught her by the arm. "You need to deal with this, Carolyn," her mother whispered, "you're going to be her—"

"I'm no good at this job, Mom. I don't have the faintest idea how to talk to a child. Tell me to whip up coq au vin for thirty, and I can handle that. But I can't...." She gestured behind her. "I can't do that."

"Did you ever stop to figure out why Sandy asked you to raise her?"

"I've been wondering that since the day the lawyer called me." Carolyn shook her head. She glanced at the heartbroken little girl, her face burrowed in Sandy's sweater again. "What was she thinking?"

"That you knew Sandy best. You two were so close when you were young, and you stayed that way. You have so many of Sandy's memories in your heart. Speak from there, from the center of your heart, and you'll find that connection to Emma."

Carolyn could barely get the dog to sit, never mind figure out what Emma wanted for breakfast. Memories of her sister did her no good when Emma refused to eat or go to bed. Memories of her sister didn't answer the questions of why Emma couldn't go home. Memories weren't going to ease the difficult road ahead for an orphaned four-year-old. "I can't. I'm not good at this, Mom."

"Carolyn—"

But Carolyn had already left the kitchen and hurried down the hall to her room. Dumping what should have been her responsibility on her already exhausted mother's shoulders, and feeling like a complete failure. She'd let down Emma, her sister—

And most of all, herself.

Chapter Six

THE RUN SHOULD have been enough to get Carolyn out of his system. But almost as soon as Matt got home, he found his mind wandering to her again. The office was closed, and he had a thousand chores he could do around the house, but instead he grabbed Harley's leash, threw a winter coat over his running clothes, then headed out the door.

Harley loved the cold, and trotted happily beside Matt as he walked through his neighborhood, then into downtown Marietta. Since it was Sunday, the town was quiet. A lot of the residents were at church, a few eating breakfast in the downtown diner. When church got out in an hour, the diner would swell with hungry parishioners. But for now, Marietta was sleepy, easing into Sunday morning. Every Sunday, Matt walked Harley in this quiet window. He loved this time of day.

It was still cold out, but as the sun began to make its journey upward, the temperatures were rising. There was a slight breeze, crisp with winter's breath, and a fresh scent in the air, as if spring could hardly wait to be ushered in, even if it was stuck behind a thick curtain of cold.

Instead of going on their usual route, Matt turned left and found himself back in the same park he'd been at with Carolyn and Emma a few days ago. That sent his mind right back to her, and to wondering where she was, what she was doing, if she was thinking of him. Unproductive thoughts, but that didn't turn them off.

Then, as if he'd conjured her up, he saw Carolyn sitting on a bench while Emma and Roscoe ran around the same grassy area as they had the other night. The grass was coated with frost, the nearby pond iced over, but that didn't stop Emma from charging around in a circle. Harley let out a bark, and Matt released him from his leash, so the Lab could join the fun.

As Matt's Lab rushed by, Carolyn turned. A smile curved across her face when she saw him, and something in Matt's chest caught. She looked beautiful, bundled up in a dark blue parka with a fur-trimmed hood that framed her delicate features. "What are you doing here?"

"Harley needed some air," Matt said. Easier to blame the dog than tell her the truth. That he couldn't get his mind off of her.

She shifted on the bench, making room for him. "Want to sit down?"

"Sure." The bench was small, which put him a couple inches away from her. So close, he could feel the heat from her body. He wasn't complaining.

The dogs chased each other, with Emma running back and forth between them, laughing. The park was empty, save for the occasional bird that flitted from branch to branch above them.

"It's cold," Carolyn said, burrowing deeper into her coat. "I forgot how cold it gets here in the winter."

Matt was used to winter in Montana, and to him, the day seemed unseasonably warm. Or maybe it was just being around Carolyn, because during his run this morning, he'd thought living in the North Pole would be warmer. "New York gets cold, too, doesn't it?"

"Ah, but the city is different. All those buildings keep the biting winds away, most of the time, and you're inside so much, you hardly notice the seasons have changed. The only time I'm outside there is when I'm running to catch the subway."

He shook his head. "I can't imagine living like that. Most days I walk to and from work, even in the dead of winter, because I love getting outdoors."

She laughed. "You always were more adventurous than me."

"Hey, that camping trip we had was adventurous, and if I remember right, you had fun." One Labor Day weekend, they'd traveled a few miles outside of Marietta to go camping with three other couples. The first day, it rained steadily, and they'd spent the time inside the biggest tent, playing cards and telling jokes. When the rain stopped in the morning,

Matt had taken Carolyn on a nature walk, pointing out the tardy raccoons and sleepy squirrels, and teaching her to recognize birds by their songs.

"That was because *you* made it fun," she said softly.

He sensed that something had shifted inside her with those words, a tenuous thread reaching between them, built on shared memories. The moment was like a bubble, fragile, ready to burst at any moment. "How did I make it fun?"

"Every time I wanted to complain about the bugs or the sticks or the mud, you would crack a joke, or point out some cool animal or tree. You knew everything."

"Not everything," he said. He hadn't known her, not as well as he'd thought. Maybe he'd just been too wrapped up in a teenage infatuation to see that Carolyn and he wanted different lives. With Wendy, their differences had come down to children. She had just accepted a job in a nearby town at a medical clinic, and had told him she didn't want to derail her career by having kids.

IF THERE WAS one thing lacking in Matt's life, it was a child. He loved animals, but after growing up with some pretty spectacular parents, he really wanted to be one himself. Scott was a confirmed bachelor, but Matt had always craved the comfortableness of being with one person and building a life together.

"If there was anyone I would have wanted to be outdoors with, it would have been you." Carolyn knocked her shoulder gently against his. "So, if the zombie apocalypse comes, I'm calling you."

He chuckled. The lightened mood brought his thoughts back to the present. "Glad to know you'd want me if we were facing the impending end of the world."

"Well, you can be pretty handy. Though I'll have to do all the cooking."

"Except for cookies. I think I can handle those."

"Look at you. One batch of peanut butter cookies and you're all *I can bake anything.*" She grinned and gave him a light jab. "And I hate to tell you this, but I don't think there's going to be a big need for homemade cookies in the zombie apocalypse."

Carolyn's cheeks were flushed from the cold, her lips a little redder, but her smile was wide and her laughter light. It could have been a cloudy day, and Matt still would have felt the brightness from the woman beside him. "I've missed this, Carolyn."

"Missed what?"

"This." He gestured between them. "The way we were always…in sync." The jokes, the teasing, the smiles. He'd missed it all, more than he realized until Carolyn came back to town.

"We did have some good times together, didn't we?" Her gaze shifted away from him, going to the park, to the dogs and Emma winding down their running circle, all of them a little breathless. It was like a scene from a Rockwell painting, or a mid-afternoon movie.

"This is a good town to raise a child in, you know," he said. "All of us turned out okay."

"I can't stay here, Matt. My job, my life, is back in New York." She sighed. "Though I have no idea how I'm going to balance all that and be a single mother."

"If you're living in the same town as your parents and your friends, you'll have that support structure."

She turned to him. "Are you trying to talk me into staying here?"

"I'm trying to give you options for raising Emma. I'm no parenting expert, but even I know she's going to need some stability and community going forward."

"Are you saying I don't know that?" She got to her feet, took a step away, then spun back toward him. "Just drop the subject, okay?"

"No problem." The words came out with a bit of a bite. He was irritated with her, irritated with himself. He didn't have a right to tell Carolyn what to do, nor should he try to convince her to live in a town she hated. He was better off just sticking to their arrangement, and letting her go at the end of the week. He got to his feet. "Why don't we work with Roscoe some more? It'll be easier, now that he's a little tired out from running around."

She dug in the pocket of her coat and produced a small

bag of dog treats. "I've been trying with him. We've mastered 'Come', but everything else…"

"It'll take some time. He's young and energetic, but also eager to learn. Why don't you call him up here, and we'll work on a couple other commands?"

She called to Roscoe. The dog paused in chasing Harley and looked back at her. Carolyn repeated the command, and Roscoe headed up the hill toward them.

The change of subject to the dog seemed to have shifted the air between them, reduced the tension. "Now, tell him to sit," Matt said. "Use a hand gesture, too, so he learns to respond to both your voice and your hand. That makes him keep his eye on you, rather than getting distracted by other things." Matt made a scooping movement with his hand. "Like that."

Carolyn did as Matt instructed, using the commanding voice that he had taught her. Roscoe just stared at her, tail wagging.

"Reach over, give his butt a little nudge in the right direction and repeat the command."

She did—and Roscoe licked her hand, then jumped up to nudge her shoulder. "Down, dog. Stop. Matt—"

He laughed, and pulled Roscoe down, pushing on his butt and issuing the command. This time, Roscoe listened. He raised his nose to sniff at the treats. Matt took one and tossed it to the dog.

Carolyn sighed. "He's never going to listen to me."

"Patience, grasshopper." He grinned. "Just be consistent, and keep working the training."

Carolyn opened her mouth to give the dog another command, then stopped. She scanned the park. "Where's Emma?"

Five seconds ago, Emma had been sitting next to Harley, talking to the Lab. Now all Matt saw was his dog, lying on the grass. No four-year-old in a thick pink coat beside him.

The two of them broke into a run and charged down the hill, with Roscoe nipping at their heels, thinking it was a game of chase. "Emma!" Carolyn called. She stopped in the center of the grassy area and spun a circle. "Emma!"

Matt scanned the park. A moment later, he saw a flash of pink, heading toward the exit. "There she is."

They hurried across the park, with the dogs running ahead. They closed the distance in seconds. Carolyn skidded to a stop in front of Emma. "Where are you going? You can't just leave, Emma."

"I'm gonna go find Mommy," she said, her little face defiant.

"Oh, Em…" Carolyn sighed. A heavy, sad silence filled the air around them. "Em, you can't."

He could see the heartbreak in Carolyn's face. The war between telling Emma the truth again, and wanting to just smooth things over.

Emma shook her head, refusing to accept her aunt's words. "I wanna go find Mommy."

"You can't, Emma. I told you that. I'm sorry, honey." Carolyn put out her hand. "Come on, let's go home."

Matt clipped the leashes on the dogs, and had them sit by his side. Emma looked so small in her thick winter coat, with tears in her eyes and her cheeks red from the cold.

"I don't wanna." She took a step back and shook her head again. "No."

Carolyn sighed. "Emma, you have to do as I say. Come on, let's go." Emma only backed up further, still shaking her head.

He could see the frustration in Carolyn's face, but also a sense of being lost, out of her depth. That surprised him, because the Carolyn he knew was always confident, ready to tackle any challenge before her. Matt put a hand on Carolyn's arm. "Can I try?"

"Be my guest." Carolyn stepped back.

Matt bent down to Emma's level. "Hey, kiddo. You scared us there."

"I did? How come?"

"Because we couldn't find you. Even Roscoe got worried." Matt rubbed the dog's head, and he leaned into Matt's touch with a happy groan. "You gotta tell your aunt when you want to leave."

"I don't wanna. Cuz she says I can't go see my mommy."

Matt glanced up at Carolyn. He could see how much Carolyn didn't want to burst Emma's fantasy bubble that her mother was just away on a trip, or back in Wyoming. In

Emma's face, he could see the same war. She had yet to grasp the reality of her situation. Matt had seen that look a hundred times on the faces of children who had lost beloved pets, and sometimes even on their adult owner's faces. Grief was a funny thing—trying to push it when the person wasn't ready often backfired.

He opted to do what he did with the kids he saw at his office—give Emma something constructive to do, to channel her emotions until she was ready to handle them. "How about we do something for your mommy instead right now?"

Emma's attention perked up. "What are we gonna do?"

"Why don't we make her a picture? There's a craft thing at the library in a little bit. We can take Roscoe over to my house, so he can play with Harley, and you and me and your aunt can go to the library and make a picture."

Emma's face brightened. "I can make a picture of Roscoe. She loves Roscoe."

"That's a great idea." Matt rose and looked at Carolyn. "What do you think?"

"That I'm hoping you're as good with a glue stick as you are with pets and kids," she whispered. "Because my craft skills are limited."

The three of them exited the park, with the dogs trotting out front in matching paces. Emma's mood had shifted, her focus now on the picture she was going to make. It was a temporary lull, Matt knew, but hopefully it would give Carolyn time to figure out how to talk to Emma about her mother and father. "You don't have to have killer glue gun skills to be a parent, Carolyn," he said.

She scoffed, watching Emma skip ahead of them. "I don't have any craft or parenting skills. And every time I look down the road to the future…all I see is a mess."

Chapter Seven

S HE HAD GLITTER stuck to her fingers and a rainbow of marker color on her palms, but Carolyn had survived craft time at the Marietta Public Library. Barely. A dozen kids under the age of six sat around two round tables, while a perky woman with cat's-eye glasses perched on her nose flitted back and forth, exclaiming over every creation like Picasso himself had made it.

Matt sat in one of the tiny chairs meant for kids, looking like a giant in a world of Lilliputians. Several of the kids knew Dr. Matt, and clamored for his attention, asking him to help them glue on sequins or color in a horse, or just admire their picture.

He was patient with every single child, managing to somehow give attention to several at the same time, while also helping Emma with her picture of Roscoe. He had a way with kids and pets and everyone he met—while Carolyn felt like she was fumbling around in the dark, trying not to screw things up more. Every time she tried to help her niece, Emma turned instead to Matt.

Carolyn watched them, blond and brunet heads close together as they added the finishing touches to Emma's picture of Roscoe. Matt was cracking dorky jokes that made Emma laugh, and she was looking up at him like he was Santa and the Easter Bunny rolled into one. Carolyn realized she had been Emma's guardian for over a week now and she was no closer to building a bond with her niece than she had been before all this happened. How could she possibly parent a child who was still, essentially, a stranger? A child she couldn't connect with, no matter how hard she tried?

The librarian clapped her hands together. "Okay, kids, let's go listen to a story while our pictures dry!" There was a cheer from the peanut gallery, and the librarian ushered the kids towards a carpeted area in the corner.

Emma got to her feet, clutching Sandy's sweater to her chest, and looked back at Carolyn with a question on her face.

"It's okay. Go ahead."

Emma nodded, then joined the other kids. She sat a little outside the semicircle, quiet and shy. Carolyn wondered if it was the new environment, the distance from the people she knew—even if they were just across the room—that had dimmed Emma's usual spark. Maybe Emma's mind was back on her absent mother and father.

Carolyn and Matt crossed to the sink at the back of the room and scrubbed off the worst of the glue and markers. Their hips bumped from time to time, and she had to tear her gaze away from watching his soapy hands twist in and out of each other as he washed up.

When they were done, Matt handed her a paper towel. "You did great today," he said. "You're craftier than you think."

"I ended up with more on my hands than on Emma's paper. You're the one who's great with kids. I just feel so out of my depth here. Put me in a kitchen, and I'm at home. But give me a preschooler to talk to, and…" She let out a long sigh. Emma still sat to the back of the group, alone. "I don't know how to talk to her."

"Just be yourself."

She balled up the paper towel and tossed it in the trash. "That's the problem, Matt. Being myself means being a chef with no experience with kids."

His gaze softened. "I meant the self who lost a sister she loves very much. You and Emma have that common bond. If you let her see how much you're hurting too, she'll open up."

It sounded so simple when Matt said it. Like something she should have realized herself a long time ago. "How do you know this? You don't even have kids."

"No, I don't." Matt leaned against the counter and braced his hands on the edge behind him. "But I have sat down with kids in my office and told them that their dog died or their cat had to be put down. When I did, I told them about how hard it was for me to lose Charlie."

"I remember that dog. He was amazing." Friendliest golden retriever in the world. Everywhere Charlie went, someone had a treat for him. Matt had gotten him as a birthday present when he was ten years old, and he'd often said Charlie was the reason he decided he wanted to be a vet.

"The first week I opened my practice, Charlie got hit by a car." Matt shook his head. "Some kid who just got his license was driving too fast and had cut through the alley that runs behind the office. Charlie had slipped under the fence—that dog always was a Houdini—and when the car came around the corner, the kid didn't see the dog until it was too late." Matt shook his head, and tears glistened in his eyes. "I brought him into my office and tried so hard to save him. The vet tech was the one who finally convinced me his injuries were too severe. He had broken legs, internal bleeding…" He sighed. "There was nothing I could do but let him go."

She couldn't even imagine how hard that had been for Matt. She knew how much he'd loved that dog, how special Charlie had been to Matt, his family, heck, half the town. "I'm so sorry, Matt." The words sounded hollow, not nearly large enough to capture such a difficult loss.

"I put him down myself. Hardest damned thing I've ever done." Matt toed at the floor, then lifted his gaze to Carolyn's. "That experience changed me. Now, when I sit down with a kid who has just lost a beloved pet, I tell them how much Charlie meant to me, and how when he died, I wanted to make sure everyone remembered him—"

"The picture in the waiting room. That's Charlie, isn't it?" She hadn't realized until now that the image of the happy golden retriever with a tennis ball in his mouth was Matt's dog. She'd just assumed it was generic veterinarian art.

Matt nodded. "He's there to remind me to never lose my heart, and to always remember that people's pets are family."

"You were always good at that," she said. "Connecting."

He'd connected with her the day they met. He'd had this uncanny ability to know her, understand her thoughts. Besides her grandfather, of all the people in this town, Matt had always known her best. Maybe that's why he had been so hurt that she hadn't told him she was leaving for New York until it was too late to change her mind. It was the only secret she'd ever kept from him, because she knew he would have tried to change her mind. She might have stayed for a while, but she'd known eventually the itch to leave would drive a wedge between her and Matt.

"You find common ground, Carolyn. There's some there, if you look hard enough."

She didn't know about that. Obviously having DNA in common wasn't enough to find common ground with Emma. There was a good possibility that Carolyn might never find that connection with her niece. That maybe she just wasn't meant to mother anyone. And that, Carolyn knew, wasn't fair to Emma.

The librarian finished the story, and the kids scrambled to their feet and dashed back to the table to get their creations. Emma headed over to them with her coat under one arm, sweater clutched in her fist, and her picture pinched between two fingers. "I'm all done, Aunt Carolyn."

"Great. Why don't we go home and have lunch with Grandma?"

Emma nodded. "Okay."

Carolyn bent down and helped Emma shrug into her coat. She zipped the front, and tugged Emma's hood over her head. "Maybe later today we can watch a movie or play a game."

"Can Grandma play with me?"

Meaning she was hoping Carolyn would bow out. Carolyn swallowed her disappointment and just said, "Sure." Maybe she could take that time to go online and scout out a bigger apartment in New York or have the long-overdue phone conversation with her boss at the restaurant about trimming back her hours, which would be impossible if she was head chef…

Which brought her right back to the same issue. She and Matt headed out of the library, with Emma between them. Matt pushed on the door and held it for the two girls. The cold air hit them with a rush, and Carolyn did a sharp intake. She bent down and tightened Emma's hood over her hat. "You warm enough, Em?"

The little girl nodded. "Yup."

"If you want," Matt said, "I can keep Roscoe at my place today and do a little one-on-one training with him. Harley is a good balance for Roscoe's puppy energy, and I think it'll help him to see how an older dog acts."

"That would be great, thank you." Maybe he could teach Roscoe to stop chewing things, too. Like the living room pillows, Emma's new doll, and her mother's sneakers. That dog needed a crash course before she went back to New York. Or maybe she should hire a dog sitter or find a doggy daycare or something. Yet another thing in her life she didn't know how to handle, and yet another reason to find a more dog-friendly and kid-friendly apartment. "Let me know what time you want me to pick him up."

They stood on the steps of the library, with Emma holding tight to the sweater in one hand and her picture in the other. Two of the other little girls who had been at the craft event came outside and talked to Emma about their pictures, while their mothers exchanged small talk about their kids. The moms formed a circle, with Carolyn on the periphery like a foreigner who didn't understand the language of bedtimes and potty training and lazy husbands.

"What are you doing tonight?" Matt asked Carolyn.

She drew her attention away from the mothers and back to him. "Did you want another baking lesson? If so, we could probably try a sponge cake—"

"I don't want a baking lesson." He stopped. Smiled. "I want to take you out. On a date."

The three words hung between them for a second. Had she heard him right? A date? A part of her heart leapt with anticipation, but that common sense half of her brain pushed those feelings aside. "I'm leaving next Sunday night, Matt. What's the point of dating again?"

Seven days until she was gone. Seven days until she put this town in her rearview mirror again. Seven days until Matt became just a memory again. The thought saddened her. But she was enough of a realist to know there wasn't any sense in getting involved with someone she was going to be leaving in a week.

"Does there have to be a point?" Matt asked. "I want to take you out, the way I should have when I was younger. I was broke and immature back then, but now I'm older and presumably wiser—" he grinned "—and I'd like to treat you to a real date. Get dressed up, go somewhere nice, the whole package."

She couldn't remember the last time she'd gotten dressed up and gone out with a man. She wasn't even sure she'd packed anything fancy, or even if she had a pair of heels Roscoe hadn't destroyed.

"One date won't change anything, Carolyn. Think of it as two old friends getting together to enjoy a night on the town."

"An exciting night in little old Marietta?"

"This town isn't nearly as boring as you think," he said. "And tonight, I want to prove it to you. If at the end of the night, you still think Marietta is dull as sawdust, I'll…bake you a cake all by myself."

"So I get a date and food poisoning?" She laughed, but already, she could feel herself relenting. What was the harm in going out—as friends only? It was a…wager, not a date. Uh-huh. Whatever it took to convince herself. "Okay. You're on."

"Great." His grin widened. "I'll see you at six."

Only a few hours from now. Anticipation warmed her, offsetting the winter cold. It was nothing more than a date, a dinner, but suddenly, Carolyn felt as giddy and anxious as she had in high school.

Emma gave her new friends a quick hug, then their mothers gathered them up and headed to the parking lot. Matt bent down to Emma's level. "I have to go back to work for a little while, but I'm so glad you let me help you with your picture. You did a great job. I think it looks just like Roscoe."

"Thank you." She lifted her gaze to his, and her lower lip trembled. "Do you think my mommy will like it?"

"I think she already does." He ruffled Emma's hair, then straightened. "See you tonight, Carolyn."

That sizzle of anticipation became a fire in her gut. And Carolyn knew she was lying to herself if she thought for one second a part of her didn't want this to become much more than a single date.

Chapter Eight

MATT CHANGED CLOTHES three times. Once because Roscoe jumped up and slobbered on him, then the next two times because he waffled between a blue tie or a green tie. He finally remembered Carolyn's favorite color was blue, and went with that, pairing it with a white button-down shirt, dark blue dress pants, and dress shoes that were still shiny from the last time he'd worn them—to a funeral.

He loaded Roscoe into the back of his SUV, then drove across town. Roscoe panted and paced the leather seat, then started to whine when he pulled into the driveway of Carolyn's parents' home. Matt came around the car, clipped the leash on Roscoe, then led him up the walkway. "You're home, buddy. Now, remember what I taught you about being patient. Okay?"

The dog wagged his tail. Let out a soft "woof."

"All right. I'm gonna hold you to that." Matt straightened his tie, then rang the doorbell. A little flutter of nerves started in his gut. He was an adult, for Pete's sake. He shouldn't be nervous about taking a woman out to dinner.

But he was. Because Carolyn was no ordinary woman.

She opened the door a second later, and he had to take a breath. She was stunning in a dark red dress that hugged her curves and dipped in a delicious V in the front. "You're on time."

"I told you. I grew up." He grinned, then held the leash out to her. "Here's your dog, a little bit more obedient."

"That I've got to see." She waved Matt in. "What did you teach him?"

"Patience." Matt fished in his pocket for the small bag of dog treats. "Watch this." He motioned to Roscoe. "Lie down."

The dog hesitated a second, then sat on his rump and slid his front paws forward until his belly was on the wood floor. Matt took one of the dog treats and laid it on the floor a couple of inches from Roscoe's nose. "Leave it."

Carolyn gave Matt a dubious look. "He's really going to do that?"

"Yup." At his feet, the dog twitched, whined a bit. "Leave it."

And Roscoe did. He held perfectly still, muscles tensed, waiting for the command that would let him grab the treat.

"I can't believe you taught him that," Carolyn whispered. "Will it work for anything? Like my shoes?"

"It should. You need to practice with him, and keep reminding him that you're in charge. Reward him once in a while, too. Good boy, Roscoe." Matt flicked a finger at

Roscoe. "Okay, get it, Roscoe."

The dog jerked forward and ate the treat in one bite. His tail thumped a happy beat against the floor.

"That is amazing." She smiled at him, and it felt like his heart lit up, just as it had when they were young and she'd given him that same hundred-watt smile. It rocketed through him, drawing him closer.

Damn. Maybe this date was a mistake because he was clearly already in too deep.

Emma came running around the corner. "Hi, Dr. Matt! Yay! Roscoe's home!" She dropped down to give the dog a tight hug. "I missed you, Roscoe! Did you have fun? I drew a picture of you. Come on, Roscoe. Let's go see it!"

The puppy trotted happily behind Emma down the hall to the kitchen. Emma started talking a mile a minute about the picture she'd made, and how she'd hung it on the refrigerator so everyone could see it.

"How's she doing?" Matt asked.

"Better. That picture thing was a great idea. Thank you for that."

"No problem."

She tucked a lock of hair behind her ear. "You're really great with kids. I can barely talk to Emma, and you...connect with her like it's second nature."

"I think you're doing better than you think, Carolyn."

Carolyn shook her head and didn't respond. He could see the struggle in her, the frustration of fitting into a role she'd never believed she was meant to fill. But he'd also seen her with her niece. Seen her concern and her patience, and most of all, seen how hard she tried to connect. Making that effort was going to count in the long run.

Before Matt could say anything else, Carolyn's mother came around the corner and gave Matt a quick hug. "Matt! It's been a long time since we've seen you."

"Yes, ma'am. Sorry about that." Even though he was old enough not to have to use the word *ma'am,* the terms of respect were embedded in Matt's vocabulary. His grandmother would always insist on her grandsons using manners in her house, setting up elaborate Sunday family dinners to give the boys experience in social situations, as if they were going to dine with the president someday. He thought of her every time he ate in a restaurant with more forks on the table than waiters in the room.

Carolyn's mother looked older, more tired. The grief from losing her eldest daughter filled her eyes and dampened her smile. His heart went out to the Hansons. Losing Sandy at such a young age had hit them hard and would, he suspected, for some time.

"I'll let you two go out." Marilyn gave Carolyn's hand a squeeze. "Don't worry about us. Emma and I have a movie night planned."

"Are you sure?" Carolyn asked.

Her mother nodded. "I'm sure."

Carolyn hesitated a little longer. Matt suspected that she

was worried her still-grieving mother might be overwhelmed by watching Emma for so many hours. Finally, Carolyn nodded. "Okay. But call me if you need me." She pressed a kiss to her mother's cheek, called out a goodbye to Emma, then grabbed a coat from the closet.

They stepped out into the cold and right away, their breath frosted in twin clouds. Carolyn shivered. "Brr. Montana winters. It's so insanely cold."

"At least it snowed a little. Makes everything look prettier. Plus, I cranked the heat on the way over here so the car should be really warm." He fumbled opening the passenger door and realized he was as nervous tonight as he had been on their first date.

Carolyn slipped into her seat and smiled up at him. "Better get in on your side before we let all the heat out."

"Oh yeah. Sorry." He'd been too busy staring at her legs, her smile, to realize he was standing there like an idiot, with her door open to the cold. He shut the door, skirted the car, and got in on the other side.

The drive to Rocco's Italian Restaurant was short. Like everything in Marietta, the downtown restaurant was close by. Its neoclassic exterior stood out against the Western-style buildings that populated downtown. Beyond that, the rugged peaks of Montana showed their snow-dusted tops.

"I'd forgotten how beautiful it is here," Carolyn said. "Watching the sun set behind the mountains...just gorgeous."

"There are nights when I stand out on my porch just to watch the sunset," Matt said. He pulled into the empty bank parking lot at the corner of 1st and Main, and put the car in park. The space offered the best view of the setting sun washing the mountain range with shades of purple and pink, like an artist with a watercolor brush. They had a couple minutes to enjoy the sunset before their reservation at Rocco's. "Every single one is different and breathtaking in its own way."

"I never really noticed any of that when I lived here and I wish I had," she said. "It's just...beautiful."

They appreciated the view in silence for a few minutes. It was a comfortable silence, the kind that filled the space between two people who knew each other well. The ten-year gap between them winnowed to nothing. He reached across the console and took her hand in his. She smiled at him, and gave his fingers a squeeze.

For a moment, he was a teenager again, parked on a slight hill outside of town on a moonlit night. They'd spread a blanket across the back seat of a convertible he'd borrowed from a friend and lay against the armrest, watching the twinkling stars. She'd been in his arms, and he'd thought the world was as perfect as it could get.

He leaned across the console now, and brushed that stubborn lock of hair off her cheek. "I like this view the best," he said. "You've always been a beautiful woman, Carolyn."

Even in the dim light, he could see the faint pink of a blush in her cheeks. "And you have always been an incredible charmer, Matthew West."

He traced the edge of her lips. "Ah, but have I charmed you a second time?"

She held his gaze. Her lips parted and she tasted the tip of his finger. He groaned, and wished they were in his bedroom instead of the cramped interior of his SUV. Matt trailed his finger along her jaw, then slid his hand behind her neck and drew her to him for a long, hot kiss. She drew back, her breath rushed, her eyes wide.

She placed a hand on his chest before he could lean in again. "We, uh, should get to dinner."

"Yeah. Sure." He tamped down his disappointment, re-leased her hand, then put the car back in gear. The sun had finished setting and the mood in the SUV had shifted along with the lack of light.

Matt turned down 1st and pulled into Rocco's lot. A moment later, they were hurrying across the chilly parking lot and into the warm interior of the restaurant. He wanted to draw her to him, just as he had in the old days, giving her his warmth. But her distance in the car earlier held him back.

"RESERVATION FOR WEST," he told the hostess, a young girl of maybe nineteen. He forgot her name—Kayley or Hayley—but remembered her dog, a French bulldog who endured his owner's penchant for dressing him in little coats. As they crossed the restaurant, Matt exchanged small talk with the hostess about her dog. She clearly loved the complacent little guy, as did everyone in Matt's office.

They followed the hostess to a booth at the back of the room. Carolyn slid into one side, Matt into the other. When they'd dated, they'd sat on the same side of the booth, snuggled up against each other, laughing and talking as they shared their usual teenage budget meal of fries. A part of him missed those days, that closeness. Then he reminded himself she was leaving in a few days, and this date wasn't going to amount to anything more than one night.

"Rocco's hasn't changed much," Carolyn said with a smile. "I remember coming here a few times with my parents to celebrate my dad's birthday, Mother's Day, that kind of thing."

Painted Tuscan scenes filled the walls, with images of fountains and statues peppered among the Old World Italian buildings. The tables kept up the theme, with checked red-and-white tablecloths and red candles flickering in the dim interior. "Rocco's does have a degree of kitsch, but the food is amazing. Too bad I never had the money to take you here when we were dating."

She chuckled. "Heck, neither one of us had that kind of money. Lawn mowing and babysitting don't pay for much. But we had lots of other great meals."

"We did, didn't we? Remember that picnic by the pond?"

The flush filled her cheeks again. "I don't remember anything about the food."

"Me neither." What he remembered was the feel of Carolyn in his arms, the soft smoothness of her body beneath his, the way it felt like they were some wild creatures, making love under the noon sun.

Carolyn dropped her gaze and studied her menu. Matt studied her. More than once since she'd returned, Carolyn had seemed almost...nostalgic. He wondered if maybe she missed Marietta and the simple life here more than she wanted to admit. And maybe missed him?

"So, what are you thinking of ordering?" he said, because changing the subject from the one in his mind was the only smart option. Ever since he'd asked her out on this date, he hadn't been sure of his reasons why—only that this new Carolyn intrigued him and he wanted to get to know her better.

Uh-huh. It had nothing at all to do with that kiss. Or the desire that simmered inside him every time he saw her. The lingering urge to reach out and touch her. Hold her. Kiss her again.

Nothing at all.

The waitress came by and asked the same question. Matt recognized her—a woman in her twenties who owned a dachshund with a penchant for eating cardboard boxes.

"I'm going to go for an old standby. Chicken parmigiana." Carolyn smiled, and shut the menu, sure about her choice. "Does the chef make his sauce from scratch?"

The waitress nodded. "He says it's an old family recipe, something he knows by heart. Hopefully it doesn't change when he retires to Florida next month and we get someone new in here." She turned to Matt. "And what can I get you, Dr. West?"

"I'm going for the calorie overload of lasagna. Thank you."

The waitress nodded, gathered their menus, then headed into the kitchen. When she was gone, Carolyn gave Matt a once-over look. "Calorie overload? I don't see an extra calorie on you anywhere. You could probably have ten plates of lasagna and look exactly the same."

Matt wasn't a vain man. Hell, half the time he forgot to check a mirror and make sure his hair wasn't standing straight up before he left the house. But the compliment from Carolyn warmed him, made him sit a little taller. "It's all the miles Scott makes me run."

"You still run? You were amazing in track."

"Those days are long behind me, but yeah, I still run. It clears my head, takes away the stress."

"Maybe I should start running if I could find five free minutes a week." She shook her head. "Stress is my middle name. Especially at work. From the minute I walk in the kitchen, it's bedlam. The restaurant got a nice write-up in

The New York Times a few months ago and that quadrupled business. There are days when I wonder why I even bother to go home and sleep, because I have to be back there again a few hours later."

"Doesn't sound like you have much of a personal life."

"Let's just say this is the first date I've been on in two years. My personal life disappeared the minute I started working there." She shrugged. "But it's what I have to do to get promoted to head chef."

"And is that what you want? To be promoted?" She'd always been driven and determined—part of what had drawn him to her in the first place. But this new Carolyn was even stronger, more confident than he remembered. He imagined she was a powerhouse in a restaurant kitchen. No wonder they were looking to make her a head chef already. "But won't that promotion only increase the stress and hours?"

Her gaze dropped to the table and she fiddled with the silverware. "Yes, but I do want the promotion. Or...I did. Now, I'm not so sure."

"Because of Emma?"

"Mostly. With the hours I work, I can't be much of a parent. Emma will spend more time in daycare and with babysitters than she will with me. She's been through so much already, and I...I don't know how I'm going to make it work."

"Then don't," he said.

Carolyn scoffed. "I don't think you understand, Matt.

There is no other option. Bob's parents are too old, and my parents are in no shape to raise a four-year-old. There's only me. And this…this is what Sandy wanted." Tears welled in her eyes. "I have to be Emma's mom, and already I feel like I'm not up to the job. I don't know what my sister was thinking."

He reached across the table for her hand. The touch felt warm, right. He saw the worry in her face and wished he could ease those fears. "I didn't mean don't raise Emma. I meant don't go back to that job. That schedule. You're a chef—an amazing one if the reviews are right—"

"Wait, you read the reviews?"

"I might have Googled you after you came home. I was curious about your career." And whether she had married or was dating anyone. All he'd found on the internet was a Facebook profile she rarely logged into, and several glowing reviews for her culinary talents on a night she'd taken over for the head chef, who'd been rushed to the hospital with a burst appendix. They'd called Carolyn the next rising star in New York, and praised her inventive and delicious food.

"I'm…flattered." A blush filled her cheeks. "I did have a few good reviews. That's why the restaurant is considering me to replace Paulo when he leaves to open his own restaurant next month. It's the job of a lifetime. Running a highly rated restaurant in Manhattan? It's what I've worked for all my life."

"But…" he supplied when he heard the hesitation at the

end of her sentence.

"But having that job means not doing the job Sandy left me to do. To finish raising Emma." Carolyn sighed. "No matter which way I turn, I'm disappointing someone."

"Then be a chef somewhere else. In a restaurant that's not so busy. Like Rocco's in Marietta." He'd thrown that out as a joke, but as soon as the words left him, he realized a part of him wanted her to say yes. To come back to Marietta…

And maybe come back to him?

His attraction for Carolyn hadn't died in the years apart. It had barely dimmed. He still found her intriguing and beautiful. A smart, confident woman who had always stood toe-to-toe with him.

A woman who had broken his heart once before. A smart man would be wary of that happening again. But he couldn't resist her, no matter how hard he tried. Even now, he wanted nothing more than to gather her into his arms.

She shook her head. "I don't want to live here, Matt. I never wanted to live here."

"Why?" It was the one question he hadn't asked that day they broke up. He'd been stunned, reeling from the shock that Carolyn was done and moving away.

She hesitated so long in answering, he thought she was going to change the subject. He waited, still holding her hand. "I always felt suffocated here. Like I didn't fit in."

"I think you fit in more than you realized, Carolyn. Just because you were quiet didn't mean you didn't have friends, a community."

She shrugged. "I never really felt that way."

"Maybe because you were too busy leaving town to notice." The old wound still hurt. Why hadn't she seen those connections, with others, with him?

"Sandy was the one who was made for the kind of life people have here. She's the one who wanted to bake cookies and get a dog, and raise kids. I...I wanted more. I wanted to experience life. To pursue the dream my grandfather instilled in me. And in the process, see the world."

A world outside of the one he loved here. Outside of them, the future he'd thought they had planned. Even now, a part of him still longed for that future. Insane, that's what he was. "And did you find what you were looking for?"

Carolyn looked away. The waitress brought their dinners just then, interrupting the conversation with questions about extra cheese, asking if they wanted more drinks.

As soon as the waitress left, Matt broached the subject again. "So...New York. All it was cracked up to be?"

She shook her head and a smile ghosted on her face. "I thought you'd forget you asked me that."

"I have a very good memory, Carolyn. About a lot of things." That unspoken thread of desire between them wound its way into his words, into the air. He was very aware of the feel of her delicate hand beneath his, the slight blush in her cheeks, the intimacy of the dim restaurant.

"Me too." She held his gaze for one long moment, then

looked away. "My life is in New York, Matt. That's not going to change."

"But is that the life Emma wants? The best life for her?"

Silence descended over the table, heavy and thick. He took a couple bites, waiting, giving Carolyn space.

Carolyn picked at her food, but didn't eat. After a while, she let out a long breath. "Did I ever tell you the story of the bird with the broken wing?"

He shook his head and she went on.

"A bird hit a window at our house, and broke his wing. Sandy was the one who ran out there, made a temporary home for the bird and brought it to the vet, then nursed it back to health. I was the one who was in my grandfather's kitchen, learning how to debone a chicken. There's a fair bit of irony in that, don't you think? The point is, I don't have a mother instinct, Matt. No matter what life I give Emma, it's always going to be short in that area."

She frustrated him, the way she refused to see past the blocks in her mind. Was she scared? Or truly sure she wasn't capable of being a good parent? "You're more of a mom than you think. And if you just give yourself a chance—"

Carolyn crumpled her linen napkin and dropped it on the table. Her dinner was barely touched, the dish growing colder by the second. "You don't get to have input, Matt. I'm her parent now, not you." Then she got to her feet and grabbed her coat and purse from beside her. "Thanks for the dinner, but I'm…I'm not feeling well. I'm going to go home."

"You're doing it again."

She blew a lock of hair off her face. "Doing what?"

"Running away."

"Not running. Just leaving." Carolyn held his gaze for a long time. "And maybe that's the best choice for both of us." Then she turned on her heel and left.

Chapter Nine

CAROLYN ENTERED A darkened house. Her parents must have gone to bed early, which didn't surprise Carolyn. At least her dad wasn't out in the workshop, sitting there until the wee hours of the morning. Roscoe roused from his place on the kitchen floor and stood on the other side of the baby gates, his tail wagging a hundred beats a minute. "Hey, buddy. Were you good?"

In answer, Roscoe licked her hand. She gave the dog a head scratch, and he leaned into her touch, groaning like he had with Matt.

She chuckled. "You're beginning to grow on me, you silly mutt."

Roscoe's behavior had shifted since she'd started bringing him to Matt. He definitely had a way with dogs. And kids. And all that interaction stuff that Carolyn felt so lost at. Put her in a kitchen with a basket of ingredients and give her thirty minutes to concoct some five-star dish, and she was in her element. But thrust her into a discussion about her feelings or other people, and she did exactly what Matt accused her of doing—

She ran.

In the moment at Rocco's, she'd been angry with Matt— or at least that was what she had told herself. But the truth was he had hit too close to her own fears and worries.

She didn't see how she could make a head chef job work while raising a young child and trying to take care of a stubborn dog. She didn't see how she could, even if she found another job with better hours, make raising a child in the busy-ness of Manhattan work. She knew people did it every day, but when she thought of childhood—

She thought of the one she'd had in Marietta. With town festivals and merry neighbors and friends around every corner. It was ideal for a kid who made connections easily, who joined in with the girls jumping rope on the play-ground. Sandy had been the one who made friends easily, who fit into every group, while Carolyn had been on the periphery, sketching or cooking or thinking. It wasn't until she'd met Matt that she had felt a true kinship with someone in this town.

Maybe he was right and she'd had more of a connection than she'd known. Because when she got right down to the brass tacks, she'd never really felt at home in New York either. Maybe she was incapable of connections—

Or maybe she'd never trusted anyone enough to truly open her heart and life.

Whatever the reason, she needed to figure out a way to

connect with a child she barely knew. Establish a life that centered around all those things the moms on the library steps talked about. The playdates and science projects and soccer games.

Every minute of the day, Carolyn worried that she wasn't going to be up to the job. That what was best for her sister's only child—

Was another mother.

Carolyn sighed. She hung up her coat, turned off her phone instead of answering Matt's call and texts, then headed down the hall to the room she shared with Emma.

She opened the door, expecting to find Emma tucked in and asleep. Her mother had been great about reading stories to Emma until her granddaughter nodded off, which had meant Carolyn hadn't had to do the bedtime routine. One of these days, she was going to have to learn it. Learn how to be a mother—period.

But this time, Emma wasn't asleep. Her niece was in her bed, but she was sitting up, her knees drawn to her chest against her bear-printed flannel nightgown, Sandy's sweater clutched tight in her hands. She was turned toward the window and—

Crying.

Not deep, heart-wrenching sobs, but slow, silent tears that slid down her cheeks. She held tight to her bare legs, but still her little body trembled.

Carolyn's heart squeezed. There was such pain on Emma's face, in the way her shoulders shook and her knuckles whitened against her legs. Carolyn wished her sister was here, the sister who was born to be a mother, the sister who'd always had all the right words. The sister who had cradled a wounded bird, woken up every two hours to feed it with an eyedropper, and nursed it back to health.

Emma was so like that wounded bird: fragile, broken. And Carolyn would do anything to have the nurturing instincts of her sister right now.

Carolyn crossed to Emma's bed and sat behind her niece. Emma's blond curls were tangled, and the front of her nightgown was damp with tears. Carolyn hesitated, unsure what to do. "Hey, Em, what's wrong?"

"I…I want my…my mommy." The words heaved out her chest, a sob dangling on every syllable. "Aunt Carolyn, can you please go get my mommy?"

Oh, God. How was Carolyn supposed to make this better? For the thousandth time, she questioned Sandy's reasoning in leaving her daughter in Carolyn's care. Carolyn didn't know the right words. Didn't know what to do.

You have so many of Sandy's memories in your heart. Speak from there, from the center of your heart, and you'll find that connection to Emma.

Her mother's words came back to her, settling into Carolyn's chest. Speak from the heart—from the memories and, now, the grief she shared with her niece. From the place that loved and knew Sandy.

Carolyn put a tentative hand on Emma's back. "I know you want to be with your mommy, sweetie, but I can't go get her. She's not here anymore."

Emma's face was red and tear-stained, her eyes puffy. She rubbed her nose with the back of her hand. "Cuz she died, like Gramma said? Daddy too?"

It was the first time Emma had used the word *died*. The first time she had begun to grasp the concept. Carolyn wished she could go back in time, rewind Sandy's life to before the car accident, and wipe away the pain in Emma's face.

Carolyn took a deep breath, then nodded. "Yes, she is. Your daddy too. I'm sorry, Em. I really am."

"But Gramma says Mommy is in heaven. Can we go there? I wanna see her."

"We can't go there, not now." Carolyn smoothed Emma's damp bangs back. How she understood Emma's pain, that ache for Sandy, for a person who would never be here again. And maybe, she realized, maybe there she could build a bridge between them. "When I was a little older than you, Emma, my grandpa died. I loved my grandpa so much. He was the best grandpa in the world. He's the one who taught me how to cook, and on Sunday afternoons, I'd go to his house and help him make the family dinner."

She'd been closer to her grandfather than her own father. Sandy had been the one who Dad had taken under his wing, bringing her along on his errands to the hardware store, or to make furniture deliveries. Sandy had been the one who bonded with Mom, helping to hang the laundry on the line in summer, or sitting by the fireplace on cold winter nights and learning to crochet. Except when she was with her sister, Carolyn had always felt like she lived on the outskirts of her family—until she went to her grandfather's house.

Grandpa Roy had been widowed before Carolyn was born. He had worked in a roadside diner when he was younger, and never lost his love of cooking. In the kitchen, Carolyn had found her calling. The preciseness of measuring the ingredients, the surprise of creating something new, the puzzle of discerning how a favorite dish was made.

"Was he a nice grandpa?"

"He was the best. And when he died, I cried a lot, like you. Because I missed him so much." Grandpa Roy, she realized, had been her connection to Marietta. Was losing him the event that made Carolyn begin to pull away from the town? From feeling like she belonged?

And would that happen to Emma if she lost her bond to her parents?

"I miss my mommy and daddy a lot," Emma said. "I want Mommy to tell me stories and make me cookies. And I want Daddy to take me to the park."

"I wish they could, Em. I really do. I miss your mommy so much." Tears burned the back of Carolyn's eyes, and the grief washed over her in a wave. All these days, she'd been holding back that tide, keeping busy with getting Emma to

Marietta, trying to figure out a plan for going forward. She'd pushed those emotions to the side, and until now, had yet to really face what had happened—

Just like Emma.

The two of them were more alike than she'd realized. Strong, determined little Emma who was orphaned, untethered from everything she knew. Feeling lost, alone, misunderstood.

How Carolyn understood those emotions. She thought of all the times she had been on the playground, and Sandy had come over, tugging her sister into the circle of a game of kickball. Or found her little sister, in her room instead of at a family gathering. Sandy had taken Carolyn's hand and made her feel like she belonged. Like she wasn't alone. Only one other person had done that for Carolyn, and in the end, she had left him. Thinking she was better off alone.

But she hadn't been. And neither was Emma.

Sandy had given Emma to her because Carolyn was the one who knew Sandy best, who held all the memories, and who could fill in the gaps that would exist in Emma's life for all the years to come. Because she could help heal the wounds in Emma—

And maybe Emma could do the same for Carolyn.

But for now, there was a heartbroken little girl who needed something to hold on to. Some stone to rebuild her fractured life from, and help her deal with the grief in her heart. Carolyn's gaze went to the night sky, and she swore she heard her sister whisper in her mind. *Remember the stars.*

"You know, Emma, when your mommy and I were little," Carolyn said, "we used to sit here, on your mom's bed, and we would look out at the stars and try to count them. We never did count them all because we'd always fall asleep before we could finish. And you know what your mom told me about why there are so many stars?"

Emma shook her head.

Carolyn could almost feel Sandy beside her, comforting her little sister on the night of their grandfather's funeral. She could see Sandy pointing at the sky, and whispering in her ear until Carolyn's tears dried up, and she finally fell asleep. "Because there's one for every person we love who went to heaven. There's one for my grandpa, and there's one up there for your mommy and one for your daddy. Those stars will be there every single night, shining down on you, because your parents are watching over you. They are so proud of you and they are so sorry they can't be here where you can see them. But you can still talk to them, and when you see those stars twinkle, you'll know they're smiling at you."

Emma turned to the window. "Which star is my mommy?"

"The brightest one, Emma. Because your mommy was a one-of-a-kind special person and I think God made her star the biggest one He could find."

Emma studied the night sky for a long, long time. Then

she pointed at a star just south of the crescent moon. "That's my mommy's star. And that one, the one next to it…that's my daddy."

The moment echoed the one Carolyn had had all those years ago with Sandy. She'd like to think her sister was watching them, and nodding in approval. "I think you're right, Emma. And I think I see them twinkling right now."

Emma raised her hand and gave the stars a little wave. "Hi, Mommy. Hi, Daddy. I miss you."

"I miss you, Sandy," Carolyn whispered to the star. And she swore it really did twinkle in response.

Emma lowered her hand and her eyes welled again. She gathered the sweater to her chest, and buried her nose in the soft fibers. "But I don't want Mommy to be in heaven. Or in the stars. I want her to be here."

"Maybe if we both talk about her a lot, it'll be like she's still here."

"Like when I made the picture for her?"

Carolyn nodded, and gave her niece a smile. "Just like that."

Emma's tears spilled over and her lower lip trembled. She clutched the sweater tighter. "But…but…I forget her sometimes. I don't want to do that."

"Oh, Emma, honey, you won't." Carolyn drew Emma against her. Her niece hesitated for a moment, that awkward wall still between them, then Emma released the sweater. It tumbled to the floor as Emma's thin arms circled Carolyn's back.

Emma leaned into her aunt, her tears dampening Carolyn's shirt, mingling with the tears sliding down her own cheeks. Carolyn tightened her hold on her late sister's only child, and Emma tightened her hold on her mother's only sister. The moon washed over them while their grief erased the space between them. And in that moment of heartbreak, Carolyn found the first buds of hope. "You won't forget your mommy, Em, because I'm going to help you remember."

MATT HADN'T BEEN prepared for the questions. On Wednesday afternoon, a few days before the Bake-Off, he took a call from Lacey Hathaway, a local DJ who was doing a drive-time radio show that would promote the Bake-Off. She was interviewing each of the participating bachelors, drumming up a little pre-event excitement.

Matt had blocked off a half hour from his schedule, gone into his office, and closed the door. Lacey started with easy questions: who he was, what he did in Marietta, why he had agreed to participate, then she moved on to the harder ones.

"So, I heard a rumor," Lacey said, "that Carolyn Hanson is back in town and helping you learn how to bake."

"How did you…" He cut off the question. Marietta was a small town. News traveled faster than snowflakes during a blizzard. "She's an accomplished chef in New York City," he said, "and I'm lucky to have her expertise."

"That's not all I heard you had. Didn't you guys used to be an item back in high school?"

"Uh…yeah." Matt glanced at the clock. Only three minutes into his allotted half-hour interview.

"And did the baking in the kitchen turn up the heat on an old romance?"

Yes, but not enough. "We're, uh, working together for the good of Harry's House," Matt said. "It's all about raising the funds necessary to launch that project and remember all that Harry did for this town."

Lacey laughed. "Way to deflect my question, Dr. West. So you aren't going to give me any tidbits about you and Carolyn?"

"There's nothing to talk about." Except for a heated kiss. A few stolen moments. And a permanent ache inside him for her.

Lacey changed the subject then, into safer ground about the recipe, then how he knew Harry, how his practice was supporting the fundraiser. At the end of the interview, Matt hung up the phone and let out a deep breath.

Sheryl poked her head into his office. "Things heating up in your kitchen, Dr. West?"

He scowled. Clearly his assistant had been listening to the live interview. "Don't ask."

Sheryl laughed. "Hey, listen, I think it's a good idea. You've been alone too long. Though if anything big transpires with Carolyn Hanson, then you won't technically be a bachelor."

He grinned. "So if I get married before the end of the week, I don't have to bake anything?"

Sheryl shook her head. "Leave it to you to see getting married as a way to get out of making cookies. Anyway, your three o'clock patient is here."

Matt pulled on his lab coat, then headed down to the exam room. He'd thrown out the words about getting married as a joke, but they held a sting inside him. Ten years ago, he would have married Carolyn in a heartbeat. Then she had broken up with him and broken his heart. A smart man learned his lesson.

A smart man didn't start cooking a recipe he already knew was flawed. Matt's mind drifted to Carolyn's smile. The way she'd felt in his arms.

Yeah, smart was definitely not his middle name right now.

AT THE END of the day, Matt drove down the snow-crusted streets of Marietta, back to his house. Harley had come to work with him today, and the Lab lay on the back seat, quiet and content, knowing his dinner was moments away.

All Matt could think about was the baking lesson he was going to get in a little while. Carolyn had texted earlier to see if he was available to do a practice run for the competition recipe. She hadn't mentioned the dinner at the restaurant, hadn't talked about anything other than the cookies.

But he still had the anticipation level of a twelve-year-old going up for his first time at bat. He fed the dog, took a quick shower and changed into jeans and a T-shirt, then did a quick swipe of his kitchen. He rarely used anything other than the microwave, so the place was still clean and tidy.

At six-thirty, Carolyn showed up, in a repeat of the first time, with a bag of groceries and her giant mixer. She was all business, distant and firm. "Are you ready to get started?"

"Sure, sure." He took the mixer from her, then set it on the counter while she laid out the ingredients. She fished a recipe out of the bag and started talking about the steps they'd take to make chocolate macadamia cookies.

But as she talked, his man brain kept his focus on her. Carolyn was also wearing jeans, tucked into short brown leather boots. Her jeans skimmed over her curves, accentuated her hips and waist. She was wearing a dark cranberry sweater that dipped in an enticing V, and she had her hair back in a clip. One stubborn tendril curved against her jaw and made him forget his own name.

"So, Matt, what's the first step? Remember, on stage, I won't be there to help you, so you have to have a good handle on what you're doing."

"First step?" He looked down at the counter, and thought back to how they made the peanut butter cookies, but being this close to Carolyn kept muddling his brain. "I mix the dry ingredients? No, wait. Mixing the butter and sugar?"

"*After* you preheat the oven." She gave him a smile. "Won't do any good to mix everything if the oven is cold."

"Oh yeah." His mind was still thinking about her touch. About how damned good she looked in those jeans. About how her smile made his heart flip. "Uh…what temperature?"

"What's the recipe say?"

The recipe. Duh. He glanced at the sheet, then spun toward the oven behind him and thumbed the dial to 375 degrees. He forced his brain to focus, to shift into work mode, as if this was just like an ordinary day in the office. Except he wasn't in his office and the mere fact that Carolyn was standing in his kitchen made it far from an ordinary day.

To be honest, he didn't care about the recipe or the cookies or the Bake-Off. He didn't want to know how to bake chocolate macadamia whatevers. He wanted to know why Carolyn kept on running. Why she got close, then distant again, and whether he should just give up on her for good.

Instead, he turned back to Carolyn's mixer, and slid the butter into the stainless steel bowl. Then he measured the brown sugar, being careful to tamp it down and slide a butter knife across the top of the measuring cup to get the exact right amount.

"Perfect," Carolyn whispered. Her breath tickled along

his neck.

He nearly fumbled a smattering of sugar onto the floor instead of into the mixer. Matt flicked on the machine and glanced at the clock. Already five minutes had elapsed—in the blink of an eye. Was that too fast? Too slow for the competition?

He turned to grab the flour, and Carolyn tapped his shoulder. "Uh, are you done with what goes in the mixer right now?"

Matt glanced at the recipe and realized he'd missed the next three ingredients that needed to be added. "Sorry. Little…distracted."

"That's okay. That's why I'm here."

He couldn't tell her that her presence was the whole reason he was distracted. He doubled down on concentrating, and started going down the list. White sugar—check. Egg— check. Vanilla extract—check.

"Awesome. Now start mixing the dry ingredients while you're waiting on the mixer," she said.

He looked over at the containers of pre-sifted flour, salt, baking soda. Read the baking soda box twice to make sure it was the right ingredient. "Are you sure you don't want to pitch in?" he said. "Because we all know how well that went the last time."

She laughed and put a hand on his shoulder. Matt's brain short-circuited.

"I have confidence in you," Carolyn said. "Besides, this is

a bachelor bake-off, not a bachelor's ex-girlfriend bake-off."

The "ex-girlfriend" word brought him back to reality. She wasn't his now, wasn't going to be his in the future. She was part of his past—and determined to keep it that way. She'd walked out of their dinner just a couple days ago, cementing the point. This was a quid pro quo deal—baking for dog training—and nothing more.

"Plus, you have to do it all yourself on Bake-Off day anyway. Hey, don't forget to turn off the mixer," Carolyn said. "You don't want to overbeat the wet ingredients or create a flour bomb. Remember?"

He flicked the switch to OFF, then measured and stirred together the dry ingredients. "Add them now?"

"You can. But I think you should chop the nuts first."

"Wait…chop? We didn't practice that."

"That's why we are practicing the whole recipe today." She laughed. "I do believe someone who graduated veterinary school and does surgery can handle a little chopping."

He chuckled. "Surgery is a lot different from this." He measured the macadamia nuts and set them on the cutting board. Carolyn handed him a knife, and he bent down to start cutting the nuts. They rolled and rocked, tumbling off the side of the cutting board. Matt cursed under his breath.

"Want a little advice?"

Carolyn's hand was on his shoulder again and the distraction almost made him chop off a finger. "Yeah. Sure."

"You want to walk the knife over your nuts."

"Walk the knife?" He arched a brow. "That sounds like it could end badly for me."

Carolyn gave him a gentle swat. "I mean the macadamias, silly. Here, let me show you."

She slipped in front of him. Unless he was completely misreading her, Carolyn was flirting with him. Was she just as conflicted about them dating again as he was? Or was she still holding firm to what she said in the restaurant? Instead of asking her, he tried to stay a respectable distance behind her, even as everything inside him wanted to get closer.

"You keep the heel of your hand on the top of the knife like this—being sure to keep your fingers up and out of the way—then walk the handle up and down and across the board." She did as she described, and the nuts went from round to chunks. "Here, you try."

He switched places with her. "Like this?"

"Almost." She took his left hand and put it in position on the top of the blade. "Go easy. No need to rush it."

Yeah, tell that to his pulse right now. He chopped the nuts, then added them to the mixture. Like he had done the other day, he added the dry ingredients a little at a time, waiting for the mixer to incorporate them before adding more. The flour and nuts swirled into the mix until everything became homogeneous, blending into one.

He slowed the blade, then dropped a measuring cupful of chocolate chips into the batter. "Is that it?"

"White chocolate chips, too. They help balance the flavors."

He glanced at the amount on the recipe, then added half as many white chocolate chips as he had chocolate. The mixer struggled with the thick batter, so he turned it off. "Done. Right?"

"Awesome," Carolyn said when he had finished adding both kinds of chips. "Now we just drop them on the cookie sheets and let them bake. Remember, try to keep all the cookies close to the same size so they bake evenly. Don't feel like you need to rush on the day of competition. This test run went perfect and we're doing great on time."

He pulled two cookie sheets off the shelf, then a tablespoon from the drawer. He dropped even lumps of dough onto the cookie sheets.

"Wait, before you put them in the oven, I forgot the secret ingredient," she said, handing him a container of sea salt. "Last thing to add."

The thought disappointed him. Once he was done mixing, she'd be done helping. And despite everything, he really enjoyed having her right next to him. A part of him could imagine them making dinner together, or whipping up pancakes on a Sunday morning.

"Just sprinkle it lightly on the cookies," Carolyn said. "The salt brings out the flavors and is the perfect finishing touch."

He made the motions, doing what she had said, but his mind kept returning to picturing a future that wasn't going to happen. She was leaving in a few days. And this little interlude would be over.

"Okay, great job. Now just pop them in the oven and in a few minutes, we'll have competition-worthy cookies." She shot him a smile. "Roscoe's behaving better; your cookies are going to be amazing. Success all around."

But when she left his house a few minutes later, Matt didn't think of success. His kitchen carried the scents of chocolate and vanilla, but he had soured on the taste of the sweet desserts.

Chapter Ten

F OR THE SECOND time since Carolyn arrived back in town, Matt woke up nervous. Not because he was going to be on a stage baking today—without Carolyn as a crutch—but because he knew this was pretty much it. Once the Bake-Off was over, there was only a matter of hours before Carolyn left town again.

He was an idiot, doomed to repeat history. He hadn't talked to her since the mini baking lesson on Wednesday afternoon, though she had replied to some of his text messages. Her tone always business-like and devoid of the flirtiness he'd seen in his kitchen. Clearly, she was putting distance between them before she put actual miles in that space. He'd pushed her again, pushed her into staying here—and what had she done?

Left again. Left the restaurant, and maybe even left town. He'd asked her last night if she was going to be at the Bake-Off and she hadn't answered him.

Matt sat at the kitchen table with a cup of coffee, a copy of the recipe he was baking today, and a long list of regrets.

Harley plopped down beside his master. Matt gave the Lab a good ear rub. "I should learn to just stick to dogs," he said.

Harley woofed. Matt wasn't sure if that was in agreement or not. He decided not to choose.

He did some paperwork for the rest of the morning, then gathered up the few supplies Carolyn had left on his list and headed for the high school. Week One of the Bake-Off was being held at the high school, with subsequent weeks at other destinations in town, like the old Graff Hotel.

And the worst part? Matt had signed on for all three weeks of the competition, which meant he was going to have to learn to bake a pie and a cake. Why he'd let himself get talked into this thing…

But he knew why. Because Harry deserved to be remembered. To have an impact on the town he loved so much. When the renovations were done and Harry's House opened, any discomfort Matt felt baking in front of a crowd would be a forgotten memory.

And would the time they spent together be a forgotten memory for Carolyn, too?

Not a productive thought. He parked in the back of the high school, grabbed the bin of supplies from the back seat, then headed inside, through the rear of the building. He sent a nod toward the other guys settling in at their baking stations. They all looked more than a little clueless.

The cafeteria was filled with booths and a handful of early spectators. Signs advertising the silent auction were being hung around the room by an army of volunteers, while others set up chairs for the audience. From the looks of things, this kickoff event was going to be well attended.

Matt almost turned around and left. He hadn't thought about all the people watching him cook. People he knew. People he worked with. People who brought their pets to his practice. He saw his assistant Sheryl come in and send him a little thumbs-up. He gave her a smile of confidence he didn't feel.

Matt selected the first open countertop. The other men were already starting to set up, most of them looking as bewildered as he felt. He sent a nod at Tyler Carter, Avery Wainwright, new guy in town Zac Malone, sometime resident Wes St. Claire and local attorney Jake Price, along with Warren Hunt and Daniel Brer. They all seemed about as comfortable in a kitchen as Matt. Good to know he wasn't alone in his abject fear of burning down the high school in the name of charity work.

Matt pulled the recipe out of the box first. He'd brought home a plastic sleeve from work yesterday and set the recipe inside the clear protector, because knowing him, he'd end up with dough on the paper and not be able to read the directions. Then he hefted Carolyn's mixer out of the box, followed by the ingredients for the cookies—including the dry ingredients he had sifted last night. A task he still thought to be a total waste of time, but considering Carolyn had a degree in culinary arts, and he didn't, he was going to defer to her judgment.

The clock ticked closer to four. He saw Sheryl across the room, helping Sage Carrigan set up a display of chocolates to sell. Next week, Sheryl would bring a basket she'd assembled for the Chinese auction, a selection of dog and cat toys and treats sponsored by his office, but this week, the fundraising came from auctioning off the winning creations and whatever the local merchants raised at their miniature shopping booths. No pressure, Matt thought. Sheryl gave him another wave of confidence. He swallowed his nerves, and placed his hands on the countertop. He could do this.

Probably.

A part of him, though, was disappointed. He'd really thought Carolyn would be here. She'd promised, after all, and he'd been so sure she would keep that promise. Had she left town? Gone back to New York already?

The back door to the cafeteria opened and Carolyn rushed in. Relief washed over Matt, and a goofy grin spread across his face at the sight of her. Her face was flushed, her hair a little mussed but she still looked as beautiful as ever. Emma was right beside her, hurrying to keep up with her aunt.

"I'm sorry, I'm sorry," she said. "I didn't mean to be late, but Emma didn't want to eat her snack—"

"I did so, Aunt Carolyn. And Roscoe did too. But you wouldn't let me share my snack." Emma parked her fists on her hips and raised her chin. Her blond curls bounced on her shoulders.

Carolyn waved at Emma, in a *see what I mean* gesture. She turned to her niece. "Roscoe can't eat people food. It's not good for him."

"That's right," Matt said, crossing the room to them and trying not to show his joy that Carolyn had arrived at last. Good Lord, he was turning into a romantic fool. This was a bake-off, not a sign that Carolyn still cared about him. He bent down to Emma's level. "People food can make Roscoe sick. That's why dogs get their own special food."

Emma lowered her gaze. "Okay."

"How about, when we are all done here, I can give your aunt a recipe for some doggie cookies you can make?" Matt said. "They're just for doggies, not for little girls."

Emma laughed. "I don't eat doggie cookies."

"And doggies shouldn't eat little girl cookies. Okay?" When Emma nodded, Matt tapped her nose. He liked Emma a lot. She was a sweet girl, with good intentions, and an affable manner. He could see a lot of both Sandy and Carolyn in Emma—she had her mother's friendliness and her aunt's determination. "You're a great dog owner, Emma. Roscoe's really lucky to have you."

"T'ank you. I love him. He's my puppy."

In the little girl's eyes, Matt could see how much the dog meant to her. For Emma, Roscoe wasn't just a pet. He was a tie to a past that was irrevocably gone. He was the one thing that straddled her old world, with a mom and dad and a house in Wyoming, and her new world with her aunt. A world that would very soon be housed in the busy concrete of New York City.

A reminder Matt needed to keep uppermost in his head, especially when he looked at Carolyn and his memories drifted back to kissing her. Holding her.

Wanting her.

Carolyn bent down and took Emma's hand. "Come on, Em. You need to go sit with Grandma while I talk to Matt. I'll be there in a second."

Emma glanced up at her aunt. "Can I have one? Cuz they're people cookies, not doggie cookies."

Carolyn grinned and ruffled Emma's hair. "He's not supposed to, but I bet you can persuade Matt to save you one. Okay?"

Matt nodded. "I'll definitely save you one. But you have to be good and quiet while we're baking."

Emma beamed. "Okay. I'm gonna be real good."

Carolyn gestured toward her mother, who had taken a seat on the right-hand side of the cafeteria. Emma scampered off, and climbed onto the seat beside her grandmother. She soon began chatting with Marilyn about making cookies for her dog.

"Is your dad coming too?" Matt asked. "Looks like your mom saved another seat."

Carolyn sighed. "That's because my mom is an optimist. No, my dad won't be here. He barely even comes out of his workshop these days."

Before Matt could press her, Carolyn straightened and plastered a bright smile on her face. "Are you all finished setting up? Once the bell goes off, that hour to bake is going to go by in a flash."

Back to all business. The window of emotion had closed and Carolyn had shifted gears. Already, he could feel the distance between them, as if she was halfway down the road back to the East Coast. He should just accept that and move on. Forget her.

But when she turned and he caught a whisper of the dark floral notes of her perfume, a scent he would always associate with her, his brain stuttered and his pulse hurried. And all his perfect resolutions disappeared.

"Yes, I'm ready. Thank you for being here," he said, leaning in close and lowering his voice. He watched the pulse tick in her throat and tamped down the urge to kiss her. "Part of me thought you weren't going to show up."

"I wasn't going to let you down, Matt."

He realized then that he had been judging her by the people they had been in the past, the immature decisions they had made at eighteen. This Carolyn was stronger, more confident. And this Carolyn had kept her promise. "I appreciate that."

She propped a fist on her hip and arched a brow. "You thought I was halfway to New York, didn't you?"

He gave her a please-forgive-me grin. "Is this where I'm

not supposed to say past history predicts the present?"

"A smart man wouldn't." She smiled at him, too, a shared connection that said both of them were remembering that moment in the high school parking lot, and for a second, his chest felt lighter.

Jane McCullough bustled over. The slim brunette was a powerhouse of energy, and brought a high level of enthusiasm whenever she helped out with special projects. She'd been a great addition to the Chamber of Commerce before she married Sam McCullough and left to raise their twins. "Are you about ready?" Jane asked. "We're getting started soon."

Matt glanced at Carolyn, his coach, his friend, his…nothing more than that. "Am I ready?"

She held his gaze for a long moment. "I think you are, Matt."

But he really didn't want to ask about the baking. What he truly wondered was whether Carolyn was ready for whatever might happen after he was done on this stage. Ready to see where this still-existent attraction between them went. He didn't ask those questions—

Because he wasn't so sure he wanted to hear the answers.

He slipped into place behind the stainless steel counter. Jane hurried back over and handed Matt a black apron. "Don't forget your apron!"

Big pink letters said Bachelor Bake-Off across the front. He could see the media at the back of the room, snapping pictures. Matt groaned. "Really?"

Carolyn leaned close to him. "Wouldn't want you getting flour all over that nice shirt and tie. Especially since you're looking especially handsome today."

He arched a brow. Had she just complimented him? And what had happened to her attitude last night, when he'd thought things were over? Had something changed in Carolyn's heart?

He pushed that thought from his mind. Her heart might have changed, but in another day, geographically, she was going to be a world away. Her life in New York was diametrically opposed to his quiet, small-town life here. As much as he wanted to make a long-distance relationship with Carolyn work, he knew better. Their worlds were hundreds and hundreds of miles apart.

"Thanks," he said.

"Good luck." She shot him another smile, then headed off the stage and over to her seat.

He slipped on the apron, gave a nearby photographer a grin, then posed for a few group shots with the other bachelors. Then he returned to his station and gave everything a double check.

Jane went to the front of the room and introduced Jodie Monroe, Harry's mom. Jodie took the stage, and delivered an emotional welcome that talked about her son, all he had done for this town, and how much seeing this would have meant to him. The entire room was a little choked up, and took a moment of silence before Jodie cleared her throat, and started explaining the rules of the Bake-Off.

Each bachelor was creating a signature cookie dish this week, followed by pies and cakes on the following weekends. The desserts would be auctioned off to earn extra money for Harry's House and points would be awarded to each bachelor on taste, presentation, and creativity, with winners announced at each event. Today's winner received a whole lot of free promotion, something any small business could always use—a free 1/4-page ad in *The Courier* for ten weeks, the winner's company name as a sponsor on the Chamber website for a year, as well as the company name printed on a banner across Main Street for the Marietta Stroll and the Rodeo.

The one prize Matt most wanted, though, was the sponsor brick outside Harry's House. Even if he didn't win, he intended to buy one of those. Anything he could do to support the cause was top of his list. Jodie introduced the panel of judges—pastry chef Ryan Henderson, fire chief Langdon Hale, as well as Sage Carrigan and Rachel Vaughn. While Jodie did the introductions, Matt shuffled the ingredients around until they were in order of usage. He scanned the recipe and for a second, panicked, sure he was going to screw this up.

Then he caught Carolyn's eye. She nodded, as if to say, *I'm right here, and you've got this in the bag.*

A simple smile from her and the room disappeared and

all he could think about was taking her in his arms, hoisting her onto this counter—

He reined his thoughts in. He was liable to burn his hand off if he kept on letting his mind derail like that.

"Okay, bachelors, start your cookies!" Jodie rang a little bell, then stepped to the side and waved at the kitchen with a flourish.

Beside him, personal trainer Tyler Carter had that deer in headlights look, all panic and uncertainty. From the looks of what was on his counter, he was baking simple chocolate chip cookies. Of course, Matt had no room to talk. A week ago he couldn't have baked a batch of cookies if his life depended on it.

The other guys looked just as nervous. There was silence for a few moments, as each of the men tried to figure out what to do. A hum of conversation started up in the audience, punctuated by the snap of the cameras watching their every move. Those damned nerves ramped up in Matt again.

He moved on autopilot, repeating everything from Wednesday, except without the beautiful assistant beside him. He preheated the oven, mixed the wet ingredients, then chopped the nuts and stirred the dry ingredients together.

Down the line, he saw the other guys doing the same. A couple of them were still struggling with mixing the dough, which kept the crowd murmuring about time and burned cookies. He could feel the pressure of people watching him, the unfamiliarity of being so far outside his comfort zone, he might as well have been on the moon.

Matt swiveled his attention back to Carolyn. She gave him a soft, private smile, and in an instant, his nerves calmed and the rest of the room dropped away. He returned her smile, then refocused on the cookie dough, dropping more or less equal-sized lumps of dough onto the sheets.

He started toward the oven, then heard Carolyn's voice in his head. *Don't forget the secret ingredient.*

He detoured back to the counter, added the sprinkling of sea salt, then slid his cookies into the oven. With time to spare.

He busied himself with cleaning his kitchen space and watching the other bachelors finish their cookies. Ten minutes later, he checked the cookies, decided they needed another minute—he was really getting pretty good at this—then pulled them out again after the time had passed. They slid off the baking sheet and onto the cooling racks easily. He set them on plates for the judges, then stepped back.

Jodie said something about the bachelors doing a great job. There was a round of applause, then the finished treats were collected for judging. Just like that, the whole baking part was over. Relief flooded Matt. Two more weeks of this craziness. Two more recipes he'd have to make without Carolyn's help.

As if he'd conjured her up by thinking about her, Carolyn rose and entered his kitchen space. "Hey, great job. The cookies looked and smelled fantastic."

"Thanks."

"I'm just going to grab my mixer and put it in the car. That way, if Emma gets cranky, I can leave right away." She leaned forward, unplugged the machine, and started to pick it up.

Matt put a hand on the heavy metal top. "What are you doing?"

"Uh…getting my mixer?"

"Not with that. With leaving."

Carolyn glanced back at the audience, then at him. "Um, this isn't the place—"

"Don't you feel what I feel? Don't you enjoy the time we spend together? The fun we have? The laughs? The…" he leaned down and lowered his voice "…the kissing and more?"

"Of course I do." She shook her head. "But that's not the point. My life—"

"Your life is wherever you make it, Carolyn. If you wanted to make it here, you could." Her words and her body language kept saying there was no hope. Why did he keep trying? Why couldn't he let her go a second time? He released the mixer, then leaned against the stove, arms crossed over his chest. "So why don't you?"

The rest of the bachelors were leaving their kitchen spaces, joining their families and friends. The audience was watching the judges do their tastings, while some people milled about the vendor booths. But no one was really paying close attention to Matt and Carolyn's conversation.

Carolyn shrugged. "I don't have a job here—"

"You're an amazing chef. Rocco's is looking for one. Boom. Job."

"It's not that simple, Matt."

"It can be." He pushed off from the stove and closed the distance between them. "If you quit complicating it with fear."

"I really should get my mixer. If Emma…" She turned away and started cleaning the counter.

Matt slid in behind her. Even here, even now, he wanted her. He always had. And he didn't think that feeling would ever disappear. "What happened to the woman who wanted to be with me forever?"

"I don't know," she whispered, the words thick and choked. "I…I need to go get something." Then she turned on her heel, walked to the back of the kitchen, and then out into the bright winter sunshine.

Chapter Eleven

NEXT TIME CAROLYN decided to make a grand exit, she was going to have to remember to bring a coat. It was cold outside, enough to frost her breath, despite the bright January sun above her. She leaned against the building, arms crossed, and shivered.

Where did Matt get the right to question her choices? She was doing what was best for her, what she wanted, what was best for Emma.

But then she thought of that moment in her old bedroom the other night, with Emma curled up against her. For the first time since she had picked up her niece and uprooted her from the only life she'd ever known, Carolyn had felt a slow twining of connection with Emma. This morning, Emma had asked Carolyn to make her pancakes, and sat beside her at the kitchen table. It was a start, and gave her hope for the future.

A future in New York City. A future that was everything Carolyn had dreamed of—the job she'd always wanted in the city she had always wanted to live in—but at what cost? She knew the hours she'd be expected to log as head chef. Hours that would leave very little room for pancake breakfasts and late-night conversations about the stars.

She started to turn and head back inside to the cookie contest when she saw a familiar figure emerge from a sedan. "Dad?"

Her father was coming up the walkway at the back of the school, hunched into his winter coat. She had invited him to the Bake-Off today, but he'd grumbled something about having too much work to do, even though he was doing the same thing as always—sitting in his workshop and brooding. Carolyn had really hoped that if her dad got out of the house, and got involved in a charity event, that maybe he could pull himself out of his grief for a little while.

"Sorry I'm late. I…" He shrugged. "It took me a while to get here."

"I'm glad you're here, Dad. And you're not really late. The contestants just finished their cookies and the judging started a minute ago. The auction doesn't start until after the judging." She thumbed toward the door, then turned back. "What…what made you decide to come?"

He fished inside his coat and pulled out a piece of paper. "How could I say no to this?"

The white sheet held a crayoned drawing of a bunch of stick figures. Penciled beneath the people were names, written in her mother's even hand. Grandpa, Grandma, Aunt Carolyn, Emma, Dr. Matt, and on the end, a boxy hot-dog-shaped thing named Roscoe, seated by a second one labeled Harley. And beneath them all, brown circles that Carolyn was pretty sure were meant to be cookies.

"Emma left this on my workbench. She wanted all of us to be here." Her dad looked at the paper and chuckled. "Even the dog, though that would create pandemonium."

Carolyn could only imagine the chaos Roscoe would bring to a crowded room of people and food. Emma's beloved "puppy" had improved in the behaving department, but he had a long ways to go yet. "Matt already talked to Emma about Roscoe eating people cookies. He offered to teach her how to make dog treats."

Only Matt couldn't do that if she and Emma moved back to New York. Maybe he could email Carolyn the recipe or something. And maybe Emma wouldn't be disappointed.

Her father looked down at the picture again. "I stood out there in my workshop, looking at this drawing for a solid half hour. I've been a stubborn fool, Carolyn. I may have lost one of my daughters..." his voice broke and his eyes filled "...but I still have my family."

Carolyn's heart swelled. She stepped forward and drew her father into a hug. "Oh, Dad, you do."

His arms tightened around her. And a moment later, his tears dampened her shoulders. She didn't mind.

Because hers were dampening his. She had missed this connection with her father, the support of his broad shoulders, the scent of Old Spice as familiar as her own name. She wanted to hold on to this moment forever.

"I'm sorry I didn't spend as much time with you when you were little," her father said. "I want to make up for that, Carolyn. With you and Emma. We can go fishing or bowling or whatever you want."

"That would be nice, Dad." She didn't realize how much she had missed her father—both her parents—until this moment. For years, she had told herself she was fine on her own, hundreds of miles from those she loved. That had been a lie. A lie that had made the distance easier.

Maybe it was the fact that she was leaving this weekend, or maybe it was just seeing her dad be vulnerable, but Carolyn held a little tighter and a little longer, to her father and the moment between them.

After a while, her father drew back. He let out a little laugh and swiped at his eyes. "Bet you never thought you'd see your strong old dad cry."

"You're strong because you did cry, Dad." She hugged him again, drawing warmth from his embrace. She vowed that no matter where she lived in the future, she was going to make more time for her family. Somehow. "Now let's go inside before we miss all the fun."

THE LAST OF the cookie crumbs had been swept up, the displays and auction tables were being dismantled, and the room had almost emptied. The final baked cookies had been auctioned off, and someone in the audience won the grand prize raffle of a night at the Graff Hotel.

Dozens of people recognized Carolyn and came up to ask about Sandy. One bad thing about small towns—news traveled fast. But it was also a good thing, because Carolyn didn't have to endure the awkward questions about how her sister was doing, and from the first person who spoke to her, she could feel the sympathy and caring from people who had known her sister.

Em McCullough, a town fixture for so long, it seemed she had been part of Marietta from the day it was settled, came over to Carolyn. "It is so good to see you back in town!" She drew Carolyn into a hug. "I still remember you playing the alligator in the Christmas pageant."

Carolyn laughed. "That was a long time ago, Ms. McCullough. And I'm still not sure what an alligator had to do with Christmas."

"It kept the audience interested." She gave Carolyn a wink. "Lord knew that there were only so many ways to celebrate the holiday. After a while, I started making it…unique."

Em had directed the town's Christmas pageant for fifty years. She was rumored to have once been a Radio City Hall Rockette, which explained her slightly offbeat approach to the pageant. "You and your sister were always so good in the pageant."

"Sandy was the one with acting skills," Carolyn said. "I was always happier in the background."

"Until today." Em nodded toward the stage. "I saw you up there after the baking was done with the yummy Dr. West. If I was sixty years younger..." She waved off the idea. "I still couldn't hold a candle to you, at least in his eyes. That man is smitten."

"I don't know about that." Carolyn shifted her weight. "It's nice to see you again, Ms. McCullough."

"Am I going to be seeing your adorable little niece in this year's pageant?"

"I don't think so. Emma and I will be living in New York City."

Em's face fell. "That's too bad. That little girl just lights your parents up, and after all they have been through, it would be a shame if they couldn't spend more time with their granddaughter." The older woman laid a hand on Carolyn's arm. "The best memories are made with family around, you know. The kind of memories that stay with you when times get tough and the road seems lonely. We all need to have those memories in our mental banks. Especially a little girl who has lost almost everything and everyone she knows."

If Carolyn took Emma to New York, her niece wouldn't have those common memories that came with being around family. She'd make friends in Manhattan, and form bonds with neighbors and teachers and babysitters, but Carolyn knew it wouldn't be the same. That made the task of raising Emma seem ten times more Herculean.

"I'll let you go," Em said. "Great job on the cookies today. I had to buy a dozen for myself. One thing that never changes no matter how old I get is my sweet tooth." She grinned, then said goodbye to Carolyn.

Carolyn wandered back into the kitchen, grabbed the mixer she had forgotten in her haste to avoid a difficult conversation with Matt, then crossed to her parents. Emma had fallen asleep and curled up against her grandfather. The sight touched Carolyn, and caused a hitch in her throat.

But what really had her choking up was the knowledge that come Monday morning, she'd be back in the car, heading to New York, and to a future that was unclear. She hadn't resolved a damned thing since she'd come to Marietta. Instead, she'd found a hundred other ways to spend her time. A hundred other distractions.

She still needed a bigger apartment in a better neighborhood. Still needed to somehow make her job more flexible, with mom-friendly hours. Still needed to line up daycare and puppy care and a million details.

And most of all, figure out how to be a mom, the kind of mom that Emma was going to need. The kind of mom that built memories and bonds. The kinds of things she and her sister had had here in Marietta.

Her mother crossed the room, and handed Carolyn her coat. "Great job today, honey. Hey, do you want your dad and me to take Emma home? Then you can spend some time with Matt?"

Would spending more time with Matt make leaving easier or harder? Maybe she should take a walk with him, have a moment to say goodbye. Make this departure better than the one ten years ago. That's what she told herself, even as her heart ached and her throat closed. This entire thing about leaving had Carolyn a hundred times more emotional than she normally was. Once she was on the road, she told herself, all that would abate. "Sure, that would be great."

Her mom smiled. "He's still got a thing for you. I can see it all over his face."

That was the second person to see something still simmering between them. Matt was crossing the room toward them, his gaze locked on Carolyn. Even from a distance, her stomach fluttered and her pulse skipped. He wasn't the only one who still had a thing going. Maybe with some distance between them, she'd be able to forget Matt.

Maybe.

"Hey, we won!" Matt gathered her up into a hug, lifting her off the ground and spinning her in a circle. The judges had pronounced Matt's cookies the best a little while ago, which set off a frenzied bidding war for the treats, a moment that still had him grinning. "And we raised a bunch of money for Harry. All thanks to you."

Carolyn laughed. "You did the baking. I just gave you directions."

"I couldn't have done it without you." He stopped, and lowered her to her feet again. "I mean that, Carolyn."

Disappointment settled over her when he let go. "I'm glad I was here to help."

"I am too." His features shifted, the elation giving way to something more serious, more intense. He reached up and tucked that stubborn lock of hair behind her ear, the space between them charged. "I'm really glad you are here."

The honesty in his words touched her. Drew her closer to him. She had missed him, God, how she had missed him in the years they'd been apart. She could feel the weight of her departure on her shoulders, the pain that was going to come with saying goodbye.

He had asked her why she was leaving, and instead of answering, she'd left the room. Because whenever she looked at Matt, she couldn't remember a single reason why going back to New York was a good idea.

Maybe just for tonight, just for now, she could pretend she wasn't leaving. Pretend they were still planning a future together. And then maybe she could leave without regrets.

Maybe.

Either way, she didn't want to leave without knowing what it would have been like, if she had stayed all those years ago. One night, that was all she wanted. All she needed.

"I'm glad too, Matt." Then she rose on her toes and kissed him. Why deny this electric attraction for another minute? In days, she would be back in Manhattan, and he would be here. Anything that happened tonight would be just one more memory in Marietta. She leaned toward him, and cupped a hand around the back of his neck. "Now let's get out of here and celebrate alone."

MATT COULDN'T HAVE been more surprised if Carolyn had hit him on the head with a leg of lamb. He stood there for a second, stunned, then gathered his wits, and took her hand and headed out of the building, calling out a fast goodbye to everyone.

He took the mixer from her, stowed it in the back, then opened her door. As she brushed past him to get in the car, she shot him a smile. "You can sure move fast."

"I had incentive." His gaze dropped to her lips. If he stood here another second, he'd end up kissing her—and much more—in the parking lot. So he shut the door, climbed into the driver's side, and started the car. The journey from the high school to his house was short, only a couple miles. Carolyn reached across the console and covered his hand.

It was nice. Very nice.

He parked in his driveway, waited until the garage door rose, then the two of them hurried from the warm car interior into the house. "I just have to let Harley out. Can I get you anything to drink or eat?"

"How about I make us something? I feel like I'm losing my touch; it's been so long since I've been at a stove."

As much as he wanted to head straight for his bedroom, he was hungry, after the long afternoon at the high school. And there was something about having Carolyn in his kitchen, whipping up a dinner that sounded really, really nice. "I don't have much for ingredients but you're welcome to see what's in there and try to create something edible."

She grinned, then tiptoed her fingers up his chest. "I like a challenge, Matt."

Holy hell. He let the dog out, fed him, then watched as Carolyn scoured his kitchen and began whipping up a quick pasta dish. She sautéed a little chicken, tossed it with some rotini pasta, then made a cheesy sauce to cover the dish. She whipped through his seasonings with deft, fast movements, then put the casserole in the oven. While it was baking, she made a simple spinach salad, then added some crisp bacon and a mustard vinaigrette.

He set the table, and scared up a couple of mismatched candles. Carolyn filled their plates, then brought them into the dining room. Matt glanced down at his, and was surprised to see something that rivaled the finest restaurant experience he'd ever had. "I think you're a magician. Because I didn't know I had all these ingredients in my kitchen, or that they could be put together like this, and I've never eaten a plate of food that looked like a piece of art."

She laughed. "Sorry. I love the creative part of cooking,

too."

He ate some of the pasta. Whatever Carolyn had created hit his palate with a soft explosion of flavors of garlic, cheese, Italian herbs. The food was as delicious as it was beautiful. "Bringing out your inner artist?"

"You were always far more artistic than I was." She forked up a bite of salad.

"That's just because I had a beautiful subject."

She blushed and dipped her head. "I remember that day."

He did, too. They'd been alone in the woods, and he had sketched her half-naked body, thinking he had never seen anything more beautiful than Carolyn. Her long blond hair covered her breasts, skimmed along the curves of her spine. He had kept that drawing for a long time after she had left town.

Then one day he'd tossed it out, because holding on to it was more painful. Now he wished he had it, because once she was gone, all he was going to have was a recipe and a few moments in his mind. He wanted more. He wanted her, with him, now, forever. But every time he broached that subject, she ran. "I never forgot you, Carolyn. Never forgot a minute of the time we were together."

Her gaze met his. Held. A heartbeat passed. Another. "Me neither."

He forgot about his dinner. Forgot about the candles. He got to his feet, then hauled her up and into his arms. When he kissed her, she tasted as amazing as the meal. His kiss deepened and she yielded to him with a soft mew.

Matt lifted Carolyn onto the edge of the dining room table, and slipped into the space between her legs, never breaking the kiss. She wrapped herself around him, grabbing at his shirt, untucking it and sliding her warm palms along his skin. He fumbled with the buttons on the front of her blouse, then parted the silky panels to reveal the lacy bra beneath. When his hand brushed against her breast, she gasped and arched against him.

He lowered his head, kissing down her neck, along the valley of her shoulder, then down her chest, along the top of her breast. She moaned, tangling her hands in his hair. "Matt…can we…bedroom…" Her words came between gasps.

"Hell, yes." He scooped her up, then carried her down the hall to his room. He laid her on the bed, then stepped back.

The sun had begun to set, its light streaming through the window and washing Carolyn with a soft golden glow. He hadn't realized how much he had craved this moment, craved having her right here, until he saw her spread across his queen-sized bed. "You are stunning, Carolyn. I just…I can't stop staring at you."

She smiled and beckoned him closer. "How about we save the staring for later? Right now…I just want you, Matt."

Those few words flipped the switch in his brain to Full On. He pulled his shirt over his head and dropped it on the floor, then lay down on the bed beside her. His hands slid under her shirt, slipped it off, revealing a soft pink bra that was nearly translucent. He tugged one satiny strap off her shoulder, then the other. Carolyn drew in a deep breath of anticipation and her chest heaved.

Matt kissed a path along her cleavage, then continued the trail down the flat expanse of her belly, pausing only long enough to unbutton her jeans and slide them over her hips. They tumbled to the floor, landing in a heap with the rest of their clothes. He teased the edge of her matching panties, watching her eyes widen, her breath quicken, the anticipation fill her features.

"I don't know…this slow tease is kind of nice. Maybe we should take our sweet time." He grinned.

"Let's do that next time. It's been ten years, Matt. I don't want to wait any more." She unhooked her bra, then lifted her hips and kicked her panties off. She surged up, grabbed his boxer briefs and yanked them down and off. Then she kissed his shoulders, his chest, her hands urging him for more.

Oh, how he'd missed this. The way Carolyn responded, the way her hands felt on his body. In high school, their lovemaking had been amateur, fumbling, but now, with the passing of years and experience, every touch whispered of what was to come.

When he slid his hand between her legs and touched the warm wetness there, she arched and gasped his name. Her hand encircled him, sliding up and down and around while their kisses became hotter, more demanding. He kept stroking, knowing her body as well as he knew his own, the memory of what satisfied her coming back in a rush.

A moment later, she cried out and gasped his name, and Matt's vow to be restrained shattered. He grabbed a condom out of his nightstand, tore open the package, slipped it on. He hesitated a moment. "Are you sure, Carolyn?"

She nodded. "I've wanted this since the first day I saw you again."

He ran a hand down the side of her face. "And I have wanted you from the first day I met you. I never forgot you. Never forgot this."

She reached up and cupped her hands behind his neck. "Then give me something to remember, Matt. Please."

"Your wish is my command, Carolyn." When he entered her, it was like coming home. She fit him perfectly, her rhythm matching his, their mouths dueling in a heated kiss that never broke.

When she climaxed, he was right there with her, the two of them wrapped in a mindless crest that swept away all thought, all time, everything for one long, sweet moment. It was better than when they were eighteen. Sweeter, deeper, more meaningful, and if Matt could have, he would have held on to that moment forever. When they were done, he curled her body against his, while his heart thudded and their rushed breath began to slow.

It had been hot, it had been sexy, and it had been a connection like none he'd ever felt. Every stroke, every touch, made him crave her more. Made him fall in love with her even more.

Fall in love?

He rested his chin on her head, inhaled the sweet fragrance of her perfume, and faced the one fact he had denied—

He'd never stopped loving Carolyn. And he didn't think he ever would.

Even after she was gone, and this sweet, wonderful afternoon was nothing more than a memory.

Chapter Twelve

CAROLYN LAY IN Matt's arms and knew she was fooling herself.

She'd thought she could come here, have sex, and get him out of her system once and for all. But from the second he touched her, she'd felt that bond, the one that had been there from the very first day. A bond she had tried to ignore ever since she returned to Marietta.

And now, she was in his arms, her heart thudding in time with his, and she realized she had fallen for Matthew West all over again.

That was a complication she didn't need. Not now. Not ever.

Carolyn sat up and began grabbing her clothes. She fastened her bra and threw her shirt over her head. The faster she got dressed, the more she could stop thinking about how much she wanted him to make love to her again. And again. "I…I should get home. I have a lot to do."

"Before you leave town again." His voice was flat, disappointed.

She glanced at him. "You say that like you're surprised. You knew I was leaving again from the day I got here, Matt."

"I thought maybe you might have changed your mind." He sat up beside her, tugged on his pants and fastened them. The lazy, sated mood between them from earlier had evaporated. Everything was business-like, distant.

It was what she wanted, but for some reason, the shift hurt.

"I had a plan, Matt." That was where she felt best, in the middle of structure. Once she got back to New York, back to her routine, it would all be better.

Except her routine was going to be different—everything was going to be different—because she had Emma. And because what had just happened between her and Matt had complicated the easy departure she thought she'd have.

"Plans aren't set in stone. You can change them," Matt said. "And maybe you should. Emma is happy here. You have been happy here for the last two weeks. And you can continue to be happy if you stay."

She got to her feet and used the process of putting on her pants to avoid looking at him. Was she happy here? If she answered that question, it would change everything. Carolyn thought of the phone call from her boss, the chance to have everything she had worked so hard for. Being in charge of a high-end restaurant in Manhattan. The kind of place *The New Yorker* and *The Times* wrote about in their pages. The kind of place where she could leave a real stamp on the food landscape of a major city.

That would make her happy, Carolyn told herself. It was what she wanted, what she had slaved towards for so many hours, so many weekends, so many years. She'd sacrificed dates and time with friends and holidays with family, all to reach this level of her career. She couldn't give that up now because it would be like saying all that time had been for nothing. "I have to go back to New York."

Matt let out a gust. "Why? Why the hell do you keep insisting on that?"

She wheeled around. It was all so déjà vu, as if she was repeating the last day of high school all over again. "Because if I stay, what's going to be different? How are things going to change, Matt?"

"What do you mean? Everything will be different. You'll live in a small town, your family will—"

"I meant with you and me."

He gave her a blank look. "Are you asking me to predict the future? I can't do that, Carolyn. Nobody can."

"You can if you look at the past. Isn't that what all the experts say? The past predicts the future?" She didn't want to go back to the girl she had been before she left Marietta. She had a new, bright future waiting for her on the East Coast. That's where she should keep her focus—on the road ahead, not the one she had already traveled.

"We're not eighteen anymore, Carolyn," Matt said. "The past doesn't have to repeat itself."

She ran a hand through her hair. Didn't he understand? All she saw when she looked around this town was the very thing she'd been trying to escape ten years ago. Expectations that she could never live up to. Friendly neighbors and long-term memories and that look in their eyes that said she should do what all her friends from high school had done, and settle down in Marietta. A life she had never really fit into.

There'd been moments, with her grandfather, when she'd felt like she belonged, but once he was gone, it was as if she'd lost her rudder. "Where do you see this going, Matt? Best case scenario."

"You mean if you stay in Marietta? Well, we'd date. And hopefully end up where we were heading before."

"Married and living in a little house at the end of a cul de sac?" Carolyn shook her head. "The picture-perfect American family?"

"And what's wrong with that?"

"I'm not a picket fence kind of girl. I never was. I mean, I'm going to be a mom to Emma, but I'm not going to turn into some Stepford wife." That had been Sandy's area, where her sister felt most comfortable. Carolyn would be the best mother she could be, but she couldn't see herself joining the PTA and organizing the school bake sale.

Couldn't or wouldn't? her mind whispered. What was so bad about that life anyway? It had made Sandy happy.

And if Carolyn got very, very quiet and honest with herself, she'd admit that a part of her had envied Sandy's life. The joy in her voice, in her smile. Sandy had loved being a mom and told Carolyn a thousand times there was nothing better in the world.

Carolyn would go to work, hearing Sandy's words ringing in her head, and she would create a new dessert or a savory dish, and tell herself that amazing the customers who came into the restaurant was what fulfilled her. She didn't need the kids and the Volvo and the bake sales to feel satisfied with her life.

"Do you think that's what I want? For you to play Mrs. Cleaver and vacuum the house every day in pearls?" Matt asked. "Or are you just using that as an excuse?"

"I have to go back. I have to—"

"Stick to what you know instead of taking a risk." Matt closed the distance between them and took her hands in his. She tried to look away, but her gaze locked on his. "Do you think I wasn't scared to get back together with you? It was a risk, a big risk."

"Why were you scared?" The Matt she had known had never seemed scared of anything. He'd been—and still was—strong, smart, confident. The kind of guy a girl could rely on, if she was the kind who relied on anyone.

"I was scared because I knew you could break my heart all over again." He cupped her jaw, and traced her bottom lip with his thumb. She wanted to lean into his touch, to get back into bed, to make this day last for a year. "You are the only woman in the world with that power. Because I'm still in love with you, Carolyn."

The words made her heart race, her breath hitch. Still in love with her?

In that instant, she was eighteen again, standing in the parking lot of the high school, at the crossroads between the life she wanted and the life she was choosing to leave behind. Matt had been in love with her then and she—

"I need to go." Carolyn shook her head and backed away from him, breaking the embrace, pushing away the clawing need to stay here with Matt. "I need to go."

Before he could stop her, she hurried out of the room and out of his house. Out of Matt's life one more time, before she wasn't strong enough to take those steps.

Carolyn walked the streets of Marietta for a long time, bundled into her coat, her chin and mouth burrowed into the zipped collar, her hands deep in her pockets. When she was young, every inch of this town had felt suffocating. But after years of living in New York, the wide expanse of Montana felt oddly freeing.

She drew in a deep breath of fresh, crisp, cold air. The kind of air she'd never find in New York. The kind of air that talked of families around a hearth and birthday parties in the park.

There were people walking hand in hand through the park, a family building a snowman on their front lawn, and the scent of hot cocoa in the air. Marietta could have been a

Norman Rockwell painting, all perfect and quaint.

It was the life her sister had loved. The life her sister had chosen to raise her child in. The kind of life that Emma deserved.

For the thousandth time, Carolyn turned over her choices in her mind. How was she going to make this work? How could she possibly work the necessary hours and still give Emma the best possible childhood?

Carolyn walked into her mom and dad's house, and hung her coat in the front closet. From down the hall, she heard the sound of laughter and splashing. She rounded the corner, and found Emma in the bathtub, surrounded by floating toys and a foot-deep tower of bubbles, while Marilyn sat on the closed lid of the toilet and watched her granddaughter play.

It could have been a scene out of a movie. Carolyn's heart broke a little. In less than forty-eight hours, she'd be on her way back to New York, and it would be a long time before Emma had this kind of moment with her grandmother again.

"Aunt Carolyn! I'm Santa!" Emma plastered some bubbles on her face, then giggled. The soapy foam popped and fizzled down Emma's chin.

"You are indeed, Emma girl. What are you going to bring me for Christmas?"

Emma looked at the ceiling, thinking. "Ummm...a friend for Roscoe. Cuz he told me he's gonna miss Harley when we go to your house, Aunt Carolyn. Is it gonna be very far away? Cuz I wanna see Harley and Grandma and Grandpa and Dr. Matt."

Her mother looked at her, sadness in her eyes. Carolyn lowered herself into a cross-legged position on the tile floor. "Yes, Emma, it's pretty far away. We can come visit, but we won't get to see Harley or all those people very much."

"How come? Why can't we live here?"

"Because my job isn't here, Emma. It's in New York." Every time she said the words, they pricked her heart like thorns.

Emma pouted. The soapy bubbles had dripped back into the tub. "But I wanna stay with Grandma and Grandpa and Harley and Dr. Matt. And Roscoe does too."

Carolyn sighed. How was she going to explain all this to Emma? A little girl who had already lost so much—and was about to lose so much more? Instead, she picked up one of Emma's toys that had fallen on the floor and dropped the floatable bear into the tub. "You missed this guy."

"T'ank you." Emma's face dropped. She moved her hand listlessly through the soap.

"We'll visit a lot," Carolyn said, her voice bright and hopeful, even though she knew the promise was going to be impossible to keep. The first year as head chef would consume every spare second of Carolyn's time. She'd be lucky to carve out enough free time to get one annual trip back to Marietta. Maybe her parents could come to New York for a while.

As for Matt and Harley—

That was a truth Carolyn would have to break later to Emma. Just saying the words, *we won't be seeing them again*, caused Carolyn's throat to close. Already, she ached to be back in Matt's house, back in his arms.

I'm still in love with you, Carolyn.

Carolyn started to get to her feet. Maybe if she started packing, this deep ache in her chest would ease. "I'll let you finish your bath, Em." She turned to go.

"Aunt Carolyn? Can you stay with me? Please?"

Her mother gave Carolyn a smile. "I'd say that's my cue to go." Marilyn pressed a kiss to her granddaughter's forehead. "Remember, Emma, the water stays in the tub."

"'Kay, Grandma." Emma grabbed her toys and started explaining them to Carolyn, talking about how the teddy bear was scared to swim but the turtle talked to him, and the fish got in trouble for swimming too fast...

Emma had an entire world going in the bathtub. Carolyn listened, asked a few questions, then sat back in surprise when Emma handed her a plastic whale and said, "Play toys with me, Aunt Carolyn."

It was the first time Emma had asked Carolyn to do something as simple as play. At first, Carolyn was awkward, more than twenty years out of practice with the world of make-believe. But after a few minutes, she and Emma had an entire menagerie playing in the soap bubbles. They talked and laughed and made animal noises until the water grew cold and the bubbles had disappeared.

It was a memory, Carolyn realized. A bond.

A start.

Carolyn bundled Emma in a towel, rinsed the tub and toys, then set her niece on a stepstool and combed the tangles out of her hair. She watched her niece and herself in the bathroom mirror. In any other house, this would be an ordinary scene. Mom and daughter, finishing the daily ritual of a bath. She could see the resemblance between them, the way Emma had Carolyn's eyes, the high cheekbones she'd shared with her sister.

"T'ank you, Aunt Carolyn." Emma ran a hand down her smooth, damp hair. "I look pretty."

"Yes, you do. I hope it didn't hurt when I combed your hair." Carolyn squeezed toothpaste onto Emma's Hello Kitty toothbrush and held it out to her.

"Nope. It was just like when Mommy did it." Emma's face turned wistful in the mirror. "Can you tell me another story about my mommy?"

Carolyn put her hands on Emma's shoulders. Their twin pairs of eyes met in the mirror. Both of them missing the woman who should have been here with the soap bubbles and the comb and the toothbrush. "How about I tell you two? Get your teeth brushed and your pajamas on and I'll talk about your mom until you fall asleep."

Emma took her toothbrush and grinned as she worked it

around her teeth. When she was done, she hurried to her room, changed into Barbie-printed pajamas, and climbed into her bed. She shifted over to the far side. "I made room, Aunt Carolyn."

Carolyn settled onto the space beside her niece. Emma curled into Carolyn's arm and laid her still-damp head on Carolyn's chest. The sweet scent of Johnson's Baby Shampoo filled the air. Carolyn's heart squeezed. *This is what it's like to be a mom,* she thought. The simple moments, with toy menageries and the fresh, clean warmth after a bath.

All these years, Carolyn had never thought she wanted that life. That she was happiest in a hectic kitchen, concocting elaborate dishes for discerning diners. But there was something so…simple and sweet about Emma's damp head on her shoulder that made the Manhattan kitchen seem a million miles away. This was what Sandy had loved, what had made Sandy smile, and what had underlined all that joy in her sister's voice. This was what Carolyn would have going forward—because Sandy would never have these moments again. The pressure to do right by Emma, to be the guardian she needed, mounted in Carolyn. "So, what kind of story do you want me to tell?"

"Am I gonna like New York?"

The question took Carolyn by surprise. "I'm sure you will. It's really busy. And there are lots of big buildings and trains and taxi cabs."

Emma raised her gaze to Carolyn's. Her eyes were wide

and curious. "Did my mommy like New York?"

Sandy had only visited Carolyn a couple of times before Emma was born. Her visits had been short, and she'd complained about the noise and the claustrophobic feel of the crowded city. In New York, Sandy had seemed to wither; while here, she had flourished. "Not a whole lot. She really loved it here and in Wyoming where you lived."

Emma thought about that for a second. "Can I see the stars there too?"

"Yup. The sky is the same no matter where we live."

Emma was quiet for a minute. She fiddled with the button on Carolyn's shirt. "Do you like New York?"

"I've lived there a long time." That didn't answer Emma's question, but the truth was, Carolyn didn't know. She used to think she loved New York, but the closer she got to leaving Marietta, the less she wanted to go.

For the first time since Carolyn had found out she was Emma's guardian, she began to question whether New York City was what Sandy would have wanted for her daughter. Sandy had loved the open air, friendly neighbors, and warm world of Marietta. Something she said she'd found in the small Wyoming town where she'd later settled with her husband. *It's a great place to raise a kid,* Sandy had said. *The kind of place where kids can bloom.*

Returning to New York and taking over as head chef was the best thing for Carolyn's future. But was it the best for Emma's?

"I'm gonna try to be happy there, Aunt Carolyn," Emma said softly, and guilt rolled through Carolyn's gut. "I'm gonna try real hard."

MATT HAD SCREWED up.

He'd won the competition, beat out his friends and neighbors with the best cookies in Marietta, helped raise a bunch of money for Harry's House, and managed not to burn down Marietta High in the process. But his mind wasn't on the successful afternoon, or the congratulatory texts and emails he'd gotten in the last couple hours.

It was on the woman he still loved.

The same woman he had run off for a second time in his life.

He never should have said that about being in love with her. If there was one thing that would make Carolyn bolt, it was the hint of a commitment. Of being tied down to anything, especially this town.

He went home, let the dog out, took a short run, but none of it erased the regret twisting in his gut. So he took a shower, gave Harley an extra dog bone for the extended absence, then climbed in his car.

It was late by the time he arrived on the doorstep of Carolyn's parents' house. A light burned in the kitchen, and he could see Carolyn's slim figure standing by the sink. He drew in a deep breath, rang the bell, and mentally practiced what he wanted to say for the hundredth time.

She pulled open the door, and her face brightened with surprise. He took that as an auspicious beginning. "Matt. What are you doing here so late?"

"I need to talk to you. Before you leave." He took a step forward, praying she wouldn't close the door, wouldn't shut him out again. That what he had felt in his bedroom just hours ago was real, buildable. "Ten years ago, I let you leave and I didn't put up a fight. I was scared back then that if I asked you to stay, you'd always be unhappy and you'd blame me. So I let you go, thinking you'd come back someday. I should have gone after you, shouldn't have given up so easily."

"Nothing would have changed my mind back then, Matt."

He agreed. She'd been stubborn and determined, which was part of why he loved her. "Well, hopefully something will this time. I love you and I want to marry you, Carolyn. I want to have that life that we missed out on a decade ago. I want to help you raise Emma and train Roscoe and learn how to make a pie and a cake. But most of all, I want to spend every day of my life with you."

So much for not saying the things that scared her. But all in was far better than standing here wishing he'd said it.

She shook her head. "Matt—"

He could see her getting ready to shut the door, to shut

him out again. He shifted closer, nudging at that stubborn wall around her heart. "Don't say no. Not yet."

She stood there for a long time, letting the cold air into the house. Roscoe nosed around Carolyn's legs and nudged Matt for some attention. Carolyn sighed and opened the door wider, which Roscoe took as an invitation to plow into Matt's hip. "Come in. I want to show you something."

He hoped like hell it wasn't her packed suitcase.

He followed her inside, Roscoe padding along at his side, panting and excited to see his friend here. Matt gave Roscoe a good ear rub when they stopped in the kitchen.

Carolyn put her back to the counter and crossed her arms over her chest. "I packed my bags tonight."

Disappointment sank in him like a stone. He was already too late. He should have known better. Nothing he had said or done in the last two weeks had changed anything. "Are you leaving earlier than you planned?"

"That was what I was thinking, yes. Get up, eat some breakfast, and get in the car." She fiddled with the folded dish towel beside her. "I thought the best thing to do was get back to my schedule and my job."

He heard the resolve in her voice. He'd heard that tone before, ten years ago. Why had he thought he could change her mind?

"I thought that was best," she repeated, going on before he could reply. "Then I saw this on the fridge." She motioned toward two colored pictures hanging on the fridge.

The first was the glittery version of Roscoe that they had made in the library a few days ago. A time that already seemed like another lifetime. The second was a rough sketch of several stick figures and a couple round brown things with legs, labeled with the names of Emma's family, his own name, and both dogs' names.

"Emma made that one this morning," Carolyn said, pointing to the second picture. "She gave it to my dad, and told him she wanted her whole family to be together for the cookie contest. The brown lumps are the dogs and those little brown circles are cookies."

He chuckled. "Looks about like the kind of cookies I'd make before you came along and taught me how to bake."

Carolyn took the picture off the fridge and stared at it for a long time. "This is the family Emma has now. All the family she has. All the family I have."

"I'm sorry about Sandy, Carolyn, I really am. She was an incredible sister and I'm sure she was a great mom." He could only imagine how hard it would be for him if his brother died. He knew Carolyn and Sandy had been really close. This was a loss that would be felt every day forward.

"She was the best mom, Matt. The kind of mom every woman wants to be. The kind of mom every kid deserves to have. And she left Emma with me—" Carolyn smacked at her chest "—the one person who has no motherly instincts at all."

"I don't know about that. You seem to have connected

pretty well with her since you got here." He thought of how tenderly she spoke to Emma, how hard she had tried at the library, how she had kept Emma's dog, even though the dog was untrained. And Emma looked at her aunt with love, and a clear need to be close to her.

Carolyn sighed, then put the picture back on the refrigerator. "My dad told me yesterday that he might have lost a daughter but he still has his family, and that he wasn't going to let his grief keep him from them anymore."

Matt was glad to hear that. He had noticed a difference in Carolyn's father at the Bake-Off. He'd always been a good man, one devoted to his family. And now, undoubtedly devoted to his only grandchild.

"It wasn't until I packed my bags and set them by the door that I realized you were right." Carolyn took a deep breath and met his gaze. "I am running away."

A spark of hope lit inside him. "What are you running from, Carolyn?"

"From what I see in this picture. From what I see in your eyes." She crossed to the sink. She braced her hands on either side and stared out into the darkness beyond the window. "Sandy was the family one, you know. The one who was always good at that. I told myself I wasn't. That I couldn't connect like she could, but the truth was, I was afraid."

He came up behind her but didn't touch her. "Afraid of what?"

"Afraid of losing the people I love. When my grandpa

died, I shut down. I buried myself in cooking, because I told myself that was the best way to honor his memory. And in the process, I disconnected from my parents, from Sandy. All these years, I've blamed them for that distance, when I was the one who put it there in the first place. And when Sandy died, and left Emma to me, I wanted to run away from that responsibility. From those expectations. I kept telling myself that what I was best at was being in a kitchen, not in a family."

He could hear the pain and regret in her voice. He moved closer, covered one of her hands with his own. She leaned against him for a moment. "Oh, Carolyn, you're good at so many things."

Carolyn straightened, and paused to draw in another deep breath. "But not at relationships. I always held a part of myself back, even with you, because I was afraid of losing it all. Then Emma came into my life, a little girl who has lost everything—her parents, her home, her world—and she's still connecting and loving and trying. And believing in family, even if it's not the same."

"Family is what you make it, Carolyn." He rubbed the back of her hand. He could see how hard this was, being vulnerable, open. Letting him in. "Whether it's with blood relatives or with friends."

"It wasn't until Emma said to me that she was going to really try to be happy in New York that I realized the price I was making her pay, all because I was afraid. A four-year-old girl was braver than me." Carolyn turned and faced him. "Emma was willing to try, to give up all that she knew a second time, just because I didn't want to change."

They were only a breath apart, so close he could kiss her if he wanted to. But he held back, still not sure where they stood.

"I don't want to be afraid anymore, Matt. I don't want to miss out on my family. I don't want to miss out on…" a smile flickered on her face "…us."

He took a breath. Had he heard her right? "Us?"

"I ran away from you once before and I've regretted it ever since. I don't want to do that again." She paused, and a smile slid across her face, lit her eyes. "I love you, Matt. I always have."

His heart soared. He had waited to hear those words for a decade. To have Carolyn back in his life, for now. For good? "I love you, too. I never stopped."

"I wasn't really happy in New York. I missed the open air, this silly little town…" she waved at the window, and the sleepy Marietta beyond the glass "…and I missed you."

"Then stay, Carolyn. Don't go."

"Staying means changing everything." Doubt filled her eyes, trembled in her voice. "And I'm still scared, Matt. Scared I'll screw it up. Scared I'll be a terrible mother to Emma. Scared that I'm not going to be what you want."

He laughed, then cupped her jaw. He waited until her gaze met his before he spoke again. His stubborn, determined, smart but vulnerable Carolyn. "You've been everything I wanted since the day I met you. I told you, I don't need June Cleaver. I need the one woman in the world who challenges me to be better today than I was yesterday. The woman brave enough to move across the country at eighteen, then strong enough to work her way up to head chef at one of the best restaurants in New York. And if you still want to do that, Carolyn, then I'll pick up and move there, too. Last I checked, they need veterinarians in Manhattan, too."

On the drive over here, he'd decided that being with Carolyn was more important than anything else. He'd been prepared to move for her, to do whatever it took to keep Carolyn in his life. "I made the mistake of not going after you once before, and I'm not doing it again."

She shook her head. "I don't want you to move to New York."

His heart sank, but before he could say anything, she put a finger over his lips.

"Because I'm not going back there. Well, I am, but I'm not staying." The smile curved across her face again, and the hope that had been a seedling in Matt's chest grew into a full-on bloom.

"You're not? What about your job?"

"I called my boss and told him I'm not taking the promotion. I need to go back there for a few days, tie up loose ends, move out of my apartment. And I need to go to Wyoming sometime and deal with Sandy's house."

"We could go together," he said.

A smile curved across her face. "I'd like that." They shared a quiet moment, of connection, of understanding, then she went on. "Finally today, I called the owner of Rocco's and asked to be interviewed for the head chef job. I don't know if I'll get it, but if I don't, then maybe I'll open my own restaurant. Or maybe I'll start a catering business. Something that's flexible enough to allow me to have that." She waved toward the picture again. "The family I secretly always dreamed of having."

He glanced at the picture, then back at her. He could see the sincerity in her eyes, the determination. He had no doubt that Carolyn would approach being a mom the same way she approached everything—and in the process, she would be a wonderful mother. "You know, Roscoe is in that picture."

She laughed. "Yeah, I know. I might need to get some more training for that dog first."

"I'd be glad to do that."

Carolyn sobered and looked up at Matt. "I was hoping you would be."

He took both her hands in his and drew her closer to his chest. Then he wrapped his arms around the woman he loved and held her tight. "I always thought this town was home, Carolyn, but the truth is, home is wherever you are. You're the picture in my head, the life I always dreamed of having."

She peered up at him. "Then let's start on that dream. I

think ten years is long enough to wait, isn't it?"

He kissed her then, long and sweet. He loved the way she curved into him, the way she seemed tailor-made to fit against his body. He drew back but cradled her close. "You know, it's ironic."

"What is?"

"This all started because I needed your help in the kitchen. And here we are, agreeing to another new start, in another kitchen." He peered down at her. "Do yo u think we have the right ingredients, Carolyn?"

She raised on her tiptoes and gave him a light kiss. "I'm sure we do. But if we're missing one, that's okay. Because I love a challenge…and I love you."

"That's one recipe I can follow." She laughed, and he laughed, and they kissed again. Roscoe barked, Emma wandered sleepily into the kitchen, and they expanded their joy to hold Emma between them, with Roscoe sitting on his haunches, his tail wagging in happy approval.

The End

You'll love the next book in the…
Bachelor Bake-Off series

Book 1: *A Teaspoon of Trouble* by Shirley Jump

Book 2: *A Spoonful of Sugar* by Kate Hardy

Book 3: *Sprinkled with Love* by Jennifer Faye

Book 4: *Baking for Keeps* by Jessica Gilmore

Book 5: *A Recipe for Romance* by Lara Van Hulzen

Available now at your favorite online retailer!

About the Author

When she's not writing books, New York Times and USA Today bestselling author Shirley Jump competes in triathlons, mostly because all that training lets her justify mid-day naps and a second slice of chocolate cake. She's published more than 60 books in 24 languages, although she's too geographically challenged to find any of those countries on a map.

Visit her website at shirleyjump.com for author news and a booklist, and follow her on Facebook at facebook.com/shirleyjump.author for giveaways and deep discussions about important things like chocolate and shoes.

Thank you for reading

A Teaspoon of Trouble

If you enjoyed this book, you can find more from all our great authors at TulePublishing.com, or from your favorite online retailer.

TULE
PUBLISHING

Made in the USA
Middletown, DE
25 April 2018